PRAISE FOI

Horror is not my usual go-to, but I've loved anything I've ever read written by Kelly Martin. She writes it in a way that keeps you on the edge of your seat with goosebumps, but without the unnecessary gore.

STEPHANIE, AMAZON REVIEWER

Kelly Martin just keeps getting better at pulling you into a story and keeping you hooked.

LOUISA, AMAZON REVIEWER

What a fun, spooky read! This is something you can read with your kids! I'd say 10 and up, unless they love a good scare.

CRYSTAL, 2 GIRLS & A BOOK

This tween thriller left this adult reader feeling haunted and slack-jawed. *What Rachel Did* is Amityville Horror for twelve-year-olds. A gruesome ghost story that is sure to become a classic!

LYNN, 2 GIRLS & A BOOK

WHAT RACHEL DID

KELLY MARTIN

MONSTER IVY
PUBLISHING

To kids of all ages and people who live behind the mirrors.

CHAPTER ONE

Jacob Mosley died twenty years ago. His creepy old house has sat abandoned ever since.

At least that's what my best friend, Bradley's, Mom told him, and he told me since he'd lived in White's Chapel all his life. I moved in at six years old.

Everyone had a different take on Jacob Mosley's demise, though. Lots of different rumors. I chose to believe Bradley's version, since his Mom was a nurse and in the hospital the day they brought in dead Old Man Mosley.

The Mosley Manor (as we called it), a two-story fixer-upper that had probably been white at one time, maybe even pretty—not that it is anymore—was the local ghost story. The house that people dared each other to enter on Halloween. The one that sat ominously smack in the middle of town, surrounded by a browning yard, falling wooden fence, and grass that sways in even the slightest breeze. The one with the new "For Sale!" sign sitting in the front yard: the only new thing to touch the house since who knows when? Probably since the ambulance that hauled poor Old Man Mosley away.

I slowed in front of Mosley Manor on the way home from school, as I did every day, and as Bradley did every day, he kept right on going. "Scaredy cat!" I yelled after him with a laugh. I knew why everyone else was afraid of Mosley Manor. I didn't understand why Bradley was.

My best friend since ... forever ... Bradley was a lot like me: intellectual, big on facts, and lover of all things scientific and historical and proven.

The only thing one could prove about Mosley Manor was that the grass needed mowing, and the nails discarded around the property probably contributed to tetanus if you were unlucky enough to step on one.

But Bradley was terrified of the place. So scared that he'd actually tried to convince me, on several occasions, to ride our bikes home another way: a way that wasn't a straight shot from school. One that didn't go directly by Mosley Manor.

I, the nice friend I am, told him there was nothing to worry about and refused to let fear hurt my friend.

Not all twelve-year-olds are as nice as I am.

Not sure Bradley considers it nice.

Tough love, I suppose.

"Hey, Bradley! Hold up!" He'd nearly passed the large oak tree that should have been cut down years ago for how badly it was messing up the sidewalk. His head lulled forward, probably contemplating how he got lucky enough to have me as a best friend. Finally, as I knew he would, he put on his brakes and looked back at me.

"I'm not going in there!" he yelled back.

"I would never ask you to." Though I would ask him to, if not to get rid of his silly fear of the place. It was just a house. Just like our houses, which sat next to each other. Just a house ... just a house.

The white curtain fluttered in the upstairs window.

"What do you want?" he asked, a bit miffed.

I took my eyes from the house. My rational mind already decided it had been a mouse running by the curtain to make it move.

"The for sale sign is new." I pointed to it, knowing that he would never have seen it himself. He probably rode by the place with his eyes closed.

"Good. Maybe whoever buys it will tear it down. Put up a parking lot or something." As he spoke, he took the time to look up and down the house. The longer he looked, the bigger his eyes became. I was glad he didn't see the curtain move. He wouldn't be rational like me. He would probably jump and run, scream like a scared chicken, and embarrass himself when I finally caught up with him.

"Better not let the house hear you say that." I pushed the pedals of my bike to begin rolling toward him. "You know what they say about ghosts. They listen."

He shivered as I passed him, which gave me a small sort of satisfaction. Chess, Bradley could beat me in. Website design, he was a natural. This house … my win.

"Thought you didn't believe in ghosts," he huffed as he rode up beside me. Even though he complained, I knew he was happy to be riding away from the house. If a crow cawed, it would have made my life.

"I don't. Doesn't mean they don't believe in me." I winked as I pedaled faster, leaving him in the dust.

Ten minutes later, we pulled into my driveway. Our houses were a lot alike: two-story, white. His had black shutters where mine were gray. His house had one car in front of it: a blue Kia. It was his Mom's, and she had nearly paid it off, or so she kept saying. My house had a white four-door truck (my dad's) and a silver Challenger (my mom's). There was a basketball goal over my garage, which had belonged to the people who'd lived there before us and that my dad never thought about taking down. My little brother's bike lay like a lump in the yard. Mom picked him up from school every day. She didn't trust him to make it home like she trusted Bradley and me. Course, my brother being eight probably had a lot to do with it, too.

Bradley had no siblings. It was just him and his mom and had been since his dad died. It was sad, but if that hadn't happened, I never would have met Bradley. His dad died when Bradley was a baby. His Mom bought the house next to mine. A few years later, we rented ours. My parents had been talking about owning a house, their very own house, for years, but I didn't think it would ever happen. I didn't want it to happen, to be frank. I loved our house. I loved living next to Bradley.

Anyway, we'd been best friends ever since. The older we got, people at school teased us about being boyfriend and girlfriend—namely Gracie, who for some reason came up with my stupid nickname ("Dorkland" ... a play on my last name, Kirkland. I wasn't even a dork. I was more of a nerd. Not that Gracie would know the difference ...) Anyway, no matter what Gracie said, Bradley wasn't my boyfriend. Nothing was further from the truth.

Bradley had been my friend through thick and thin over the last six years. We were neighbors. We were inseparable. We were—

"Ava! I'm glad you're home!" my mother yelled from the porch. "I have amazing news! We just bought the Mosley place! We will finally be homeowners!"

Bradley wobbled back a bit, catching himself on his bike for support. I looked at him. His face had turned an ashy white. "M-Mosley Manor? With the g-ghosts?"

This wasn't good.

Not good at all.

CHAPTER TWO

We pulled up to Mosley Manor a quarter past ten in the morning, and already it looked dead. Dead, meaning that there was sunshine on all the other houses along the street, but not this one. This one was covered with an ominous gray shadow. I hadn't ever noticed that before on our many, many trips by it during the school year.

It was the last Saturday before summer break and, my lucky stars, I was at my new house.

"Isn't it something?" Mama asked as she jumped out of the driver's seat.

"It's something alright," I mumbled, low enough that she couldn't hear me. Ever since I was told about the house, I tried my best not to grumble too much. What could I say? That I didn't want to move into the haunted old place? I didn't even believe it was haunted. Bradley would have laughed me out of the neighborhood.

I missed being his neighbor already, but as my parents kept telling me, it wasn't like we'd moved to Mars. Bradley was literally still five minutes from my house. We could visit anytime.

I was ready to go and visit him now.

The white curtain in the second-floor window shifted to the side, catching my eye. With my luck, that would be my room. The one with the mouse problem.

My dad jumped out of the passenger's side with a big smile beneath his graying beard. "It's perfect."

"Perfect for Dracula," my little brother, Evan, squealed as he popped out behind me. Evan was four years younger and seven times more annoying than me.

"Oh, hush." Mama laughed as she wrapped her arm around my dad's waist. Ewww … My parents did that, show affection a little—read: a lot—too much. They were always holding hands, stealing kisses, hugging, giggling—things old people should not do. "Your dad's right. It's perfect."

My definition of perfect must have been wrong.

Mosley Manor had been fun to tease Bradley about, but now that I had to live there, it wasn't so fun. Looking at it, I noticed how off-kilter it looked, like it leaned on its foundation just enough for a funhouse effect. The tall grass in the front of the house blew steadily, and it occurred to me, there was no wind to force it to move at the moment.

The gate squeaked, breaking me from my mini-breakdown. "Let's check out the inside. I bet it has some amazing bones." Mama sounded positively giddy.

"Skeleton bones." Evan rolled his eyes and hit my arm as he skipped toward the house.

Go inside … go inside! I had forgotten that I would have to actually go in there. I supposed I'd just stand there and look at it forever.

My parents and Evan disappeared into the old house before I even took a step. I bent my ear and listened, trying to hear any out-of-place sounds.

Was I a hypocrite? Yes, yes, I was. If Bradley had been with me, I would have made fun of him awful. As it was, he had to go to Nashville with his mom that morning, so I was safe from his judgment and laughter. Though I could have used the moral support.

The white curtain on the second floor shifted again. This time, it was a bigger movement, one that immediately caught my eye and made me jump. I balled my fingers into a fist and tried my hardest not to freak out. It was a house, a stupid house. There weren't any ghosts, and I needed to …

A head popped up in the window. A pale face with big blue eyes, mouth open in a scream.

I jumped back, landing against the truck. My knees wobbled, and I had to grab the door for support. If words would have come out, I would have scared the crows sitting on the dead tree branches on the house. As it were, they just looked at me like I was crazy.

Laughter brought me out of my irrational, freaked-out, induced state. Laughter from the top window.

It had been a pale face, all right: the pale face of Evan. He stuck his finger out, pointing at my silliness. Then he doubled over, obviously enjoying how much he'd scared his non-scare-able big sister.

"I'm going to get you," I mouthed at him.

Without thinking, without a second thought, I let my sisterly anger take over; I ran through the gate, up the steps, and into the house without hesitation. Oh, Evan would pay, all right. It was on.

The inside of the house was … not bad, actually. At least the ceiling wasn't falling down. In front of me, a fairly sturdy-looking staircase twisted up to the second floor. Cream and gold wallpaper with a design that reminded me of something I'd seen in a history book from the nineteen-twenties era reached from floor to ceiling. As a history buff, I appreciated the history in the house, and it occurred to me that I'd been thinking about this all wrong. This wasn't a scary house. Of course, it wasn't full of ghosts—which didn't exist. The house was a history person's dream. There was no telling what sorts of historical pieces I could find here.

It was enough to make me giddy.

My first thoughts of the layout of the house were that whoever built it certainly didn't know about an open floor plan. I stood in the foyer. To my right was what I assumed was a dining room. The windows were boarded up, so I couldn't totally tell from where I stood. I thought I saw the legs of a dining table in the middle of the room. To my left, a fireplace let me know that room had been the living room.

I hoped Mr. Mosley had at least found the luxury of modern indoor plumbing to be beneficial. Lots of dust laid on the sheets covering what I assumed was Jacob Mosley's furniture. He'd died without any relatives, or so I'd heard, so it made sense everything remained here. Who had sold the house? Who had my parents bought it from?

Where was Evan so I could sit on him?

I ran up the stairs, each one creaking under me. I didn't stop until I reached the second floor.

Evan was nowhere to be found.

CHAPTER THREE

"Evan!" I opened the second door on my right, expecting him to jump out at me, and scare me like he'd wanted to all day.

What I found was a bathroom that had seen better days with a window open at the far side of the room, the curtain flapping in the warm May breeze. There was a claw-foot tub, which looked pretty grimy. The walls were black and off-white tile. The sink sat at a precarious angle, and the toilet had a pea-green toilet brush standing on top of it.

Such a lovely ... lovely room.

I nearly gagged, thinking about how this would be where I'd have to actually spend some quality time—just like this—until whenever my parents got around to fixing it up.

My parents had talked about owning their own house for as long as I could remember, but was this house that much superior to our old house? Cause not to me.

I'd take our rental house any day.

I already missed Bradley, even though I'd see him Monday for the last day of school before summer break.

The one person I didn't miss was ... "Evan!" I left the

bathroom door open and marched into the hallway. I wasn't in the mood to chase after him all day.

The door at the far end of the hallway sat slightly ajar, so I rammed it open with my shoulder, and to my enjoyment, Evan's whiney voice screeched, "Ouch!"

Ha, found him.

"What are you doing, hiding up here? You can't get out of unpacking that easily." I crossed my arms, examining him as he withdrew his fingers from his nose a few times. If it was broken, my parents would kill me. Thankfully, after the second dab and no blood came off, I knew I was home free.

"One, you didn't have to hit me," he countered.

"I didn't hit you. The door did," I corrected him with a smirk.

He glared at me like he didn't think it was as funny as I did. "And two, I wasn't hiding. I was being friendly."

Sometimes my brother said weird stuff … like that he loves me, or that the sky is orange, or that he's being friendly in an obviously empty room.

I took the time to fully examine the room he had hunkered down in. A four-poster bed stood in the middle of the room; its posts nearly scraped the ceiling. A quilt in a "wedding ring" design sprawled out across the mattress like it had been made yesterday. I knew the term "wedding ring" when it came to quilts because my grandmother taught me. She even tried to show me how to sew and quilt, but my fingers weren't coordinated, and I failed, miserably, every time.

The window to the room remained closed, not like the one in the bathroom, which had been odd. How long had it been open? How did rain not seep in and rot the floor?

So many questions … "Are you listening to me?" Evan whined, bringing me back to our conversation.

"Not really," I admitted and spun on my heel. "We need

to get downstairs and help bring our stuff in. I call dibs on this room. You can have the one across the hall from the bathroom."

Evan sat up straighter and shook his head. "No, you take that one. I want this one."

"Why? To be friendly?" I rolled my eyes with as much sarcasm as I could muster.

Evan simply looked to his left, then back at me. "I just think you'd like the other room better. That's all."

"So, you're thinking of me?" I scoffed.

But when Evan nodded, I don't know, something inside me believed him. "We want you to have it."

Wait … "We?"

"Me. I mean me. I … uh … I want you to have it. Not we. Why would I say 'we'? That would be … crazy."

I shook my head and sighed. "Fine, Evan. Fine. You take this room. I'll take the one in front of the bathroom." The one with the mouse problem—I finish in my head.

"Thanks. We owe you." He hugged me tighter than he had since we were little. Before I could fully comprehend what he was doing, he shut the door between us.

That was that.

"Weirdo," I mumbled to myself.

My stomach ached just thinking about having to stay in that creepy bedroom across the hallway from the bathroom. Not because of ghosts or monsters—I was too mature to believe in such things. But because of the mice that had moved the curtains not once, but twice. No telling how many had infested the room, made it their own little home. If it had furniture in it, it would have to go, like today, tomorrow at the latest. No way was I bunking with rodents.

I threw my shoulders back and started for my new (read: ancient) room, when something caught my eye. I halted and examined the hallway. Something wasn't right. Something felt … off. Downstairs, I heard my parents bringing in boxes. My mom laughed at something my dad said. Then it got quiet. I imagined there was some sort of kissing, which made me kinda sick. I was glad they still loved each other after fifteen years, but did they have to kiss every five seconds to prove it?

From where I stood, I could see every door upstairs. Behind me was Evan's newly claimed room. Two doors away was my room. Between our rooms was a door I hadn't opened yet and didn't want to open. At the far end of the hallway was another unopened door. And of course, the bathroom was across the hall from my room, and the door had been left open …

The door … had been left open.

The bathroom door …

I blinked slowly, praying my eyes were simply playing tricks on me. I was tired. I was upset after losing my preferred room to my younger brother … I must have forgotten.

The bathroom door was closed.

It hadn't slammed.

It hadn't been shut.

And I knew I'd opened it.

"Must have been the wind from the open window," I told myself. It had to be that. There was no other explanation.

Not wanting to be alone anymore, though, I ran downstairs and found, not in the least to my surprise, Mama and Daddy embracing in the living room, slow dancing to music only in their heads. Thank goodness they weren't kissing, though. I could only take so much.

"I don't like this house," I announced to anyone who would listen, which was neither of them.

Once I saw my protest fall on deaf ears, I marched myself out of the house through the front door, ran down the porch steps, and didn't stop until I had reached the sidewalk. I breathed the fresh, non-moldy air, and allowed the warm sunshine to engulf me. I was being completely stupid about the house. Everything I'd seen had a reasonable explanation.

A mouse moved the curtain in my unfortunate room … twice.

The wind shut the bathroom door.

My brother had misspoken when he said 'we' earlier.

Everything was fine.

I believed it until I saw Bradley sitting on the sidewalk with his back to the fence, his knees drawn to his chest. He looked terrified.

CHAPTER FOUR

I t took me a minute to register that Bradley was, in fact, here, sitting on the ground, terrified. It must have taken him a second to register I was there as well. First, he noticed my shoes, and slowly, his eyes scanned my knees and my belly until they landed on my face. He sighed when he saw it was me and instantly wiped the tears away.

Tears. Why was he crying?

"Sorry … I'm sorry." Bradley scooted up to his knees and wiped the dirt from his bottom.

I reached down to help him up, but he ignored my hand and stood, leaning on the fence, with his back to me. I could see how heavy he was breathing and wondered for a second if he was dying or something.

"What's wrong?" I asked, seriously about to run inside and get my mom and dad to help.

He shook his head and took a deep breath. "Nothing. I just …"

Nothing good ever came from 'nothing.'

I patted his shoulder to get him to turn around and see

me. That was the wrong move, however. He jumped like he saw a jumpscare in a video game. "Sorry ... I'm so sorry."

"You keep saying that. Let me get my mom, okay? Stay right here."

I started to walk away when he started talking. "I saw it."

"You saw what?"

"I saw, or I thought I saw, something in the upstairs window."

Bradley closed his eyes, I assumed to get some sort of composure and sucked in a big breath. He opened his eyes as he breathed out slowly. He looked bad, like really bad. Besides, his hair all flopped over his head, sweat beaded on his forehead, his face was pale, and his lips were so white they faded into the rest of the skin on his face. It was a face I'd seen on his mom a few times when life overwhelmed her.

I tried very hard not to laugh. Bradley was my best friend after all, and it would have been very rude to laugh at how upset something so minor had made him. "That was a mouse." I hiccuped back a giggle.

His eyebrow rose the way it did when we were in class, and there was a difficult math problem on the board. I could see the figurative wheels in his head turning.

"A mouse," I repeated. "In that window. I've seen the curtain move twice now. It was just a little mouse. Nothing to be scared of." I felt pretty brave at the moment. Sure, I'd been a bit terrified a few minutes before, but Bradley didn't have to know that. The house was my chess, after all. My win.

"A mouse." He tilted his head like he didn't quite believe me.

"A mouse," I repeated again, a tad more slowly to get my point across. "Just a mouse. A tiny, little mouse, running across the windowsill. Nothing more. And yeah, sure, it's gross to have a mouse in your room with all the yucky drop-pings they leave behind, but still … it beats the alternative."

"The alternative, as in, ghost?"

He wanted me to say that I believed in ghosts. It would have probably made him feel better. But despite my freak-out, I didn't believe in ghosts. Not in the slightest. There was no scientific evidence to prove they existed; therefore, they didn't exist. "Bradley, the only truly terrifying thing in that house is my little brother," I said with a laugh. I hope he got my meaning, though.

He nodded. Color came to his cheeks, and he looked much less pale.

I let out the breath I hadn't realized I'd been holding and patted him on the shoulder. "Come on. Want to see inside Mosley Manor?"

Bradley shook his head and ran his fingers through his dark-brown hair. He hadn't had it cut all school year, and, much to his mom's chagrin, it had curled around his ears in messy waves. I honestly hadn't noticed how much it had grown until Gracie Redding—a gawker of Bradley's, a self-proclaimed "fearless" person, and a sniffer of dry erase markers—mentioned it at school one day. Gracie had also been my tormentor for years and thought she was hilarious for coming up with my nickname, Dorkland.

Anyway, Gracie thought Bradley was, in her word, "hot." I never told him that. I didn't want him to think I thought it too … which I didn't.

"I can't believe this is your new house." Bradley stared up at the house like it would bite him.

"Me neither." I'd probably get used to it. I mean, I loved history, and this house had plenty of it. Take away the fact that it was falling down, and there was a lot to like about the house. If I told myself that enough, maybe I'd start to believe it. "Sure you don't want to come in? I promise, it's only a house."

He glared down at me. "Only a house that is made up of my nightmares."

"Well, yeah. That too."

"Maybe tomorrow," he said in a tone that made me think it most certainly wouldn't be tomorrow. "I gotta go." He looked like someone had kicked him as he bent down and grabbed his bike.

He walked the bike away as I yelled, "I'll see you Monday."

Bradley stopped long enough to turn around and slowly nod.

As I watched him get smaller and smaller, I had a newfound dislike for my new house. It being full of mice and the neighborhood haunted house was one thing. I kinda liked that about it—the haunted-history part, not the mice part— but for it to scare my best friend into not wanting to come back, I might not ever be able to forgive it.

Once Bradley got so far away I couldn't see him anymore, I stomped right up the crumbling walkway, up the rickety steps, and slammed the wobbly front door behind me loud enough for my parents to jump.

"This house stinks." And I didn't mean from the mold and decay.

Without waiting for them to reply, I ran upstairs and didn't stop until I was in my new room, my face stuffed into a pillow that probably hadn't been fluffed or cleaned since the Kennedy administration.

Everyone needed to get a grip about this house. Especially Bradley. Of course, part of it was my own fault. I'm the one who liked to scare him about the house … everyday … as we went passed it. Time for all that was over. I wouldn't lose my best friend over a stupid house. I knew what I had to do.

Somehow, I had to make the scariest house in town not so scary.

CHAPTER FIVE

Considering I woke up at three in the morning, waking up for the last day of school didn't stink. I meant that in the most sarcastic of ways.

Being woken up by your little brother standing over you, watching you sleep was, in a word, weird. I asked him what he wanted. He didn't say a word. I turned on the light, and he blinked a few times, like waking up from a dream. After that, he turned and went out my door and, I assume, back to his room.

Of all the things happening, I didn't need my brother being weird as part of it.

The next morning, I brushed my teeth as quickly as I could in the falling down, needing renovation bathroom in front of my room and went to find some clothes for school. I knew we wouldn't do much in class. All end-of-year tests had been given, and all kids fifth through eighth grade had the option of staying home, but as an incentive to come, on the last day of every year, the school hosted a big dodgeball tournament. I was a dodgeball champion, which surprised most of the class, being the nerdy girl I am. It even surprised

Bradley, who didn't like dodgeball, but played because I loved it.

So, of course, I had every intention of going to school today. I hoped Bradley kept his promise and came, too. I wanted to talk to him about Saturday. Tell him I survived the weekend with no incidents (I refused to tell him about my weirdo brother), and how the house really wasn't that bad. I needed him to be okay with the house so he could come over and visit during the summer. I figured if worse came to worse, I could just spend every summer day at his house, but he had the meanest babysitter ever and, well … I'd endure it if I had to.

I threw my black shorts and matching shirt on, tossed my curls into what would have to pass for a ponytail, put on my most comfortable sneakers, and headed out of my room to face the day with a brand new, positive attitude.

First thing I noticed was the bathroom door was shut. Had I done that? I thought I'd left it open, but I could have been mistaken. It wasn't like I was going to think about it too much.

Positivity.

It was the name of the day.

I pounded on Evan's door to make sure he was up. I didn't want him to make me late.

"Shhhhh …" he said before he door opened. He looked as tired as I felt.

"Don't 'shhhh' me." I crossed my arms and gave him the older-sister glare.

"What? No, I'm not shhhing you. I'm … you know, never mind. Let's go."

My brother had on the exact same clothes he'd had on the day before. His hair was all tousled, and he had black bags under his eyes.

"I didn't sleep well," he commented without me having to say a word.

"You don't say. Maybe you would have if you hadn't been staring me down this morning."

"What? When?" A thud echoed through his room, and before I could look around to see what it was, Evan slammed the door in my face. "Mouse," he said.

"Uh-huh. Mouse." I felt like Bradley must have felt when I told him the same thing. Poor rodents, blamed for everything. "Look, you don't have some sort of pet in there, do you? An illegal iguana or something?"

Evan gave a nervous laugh and turned me toward the stairs. "I wish. No, just new house jitters, that's all. We haven't moved in so long. It'll take some getting used to."

That was one thing I could agree on. "I bet Mama and Daddy have already adjusted." Because I was a good big sister, I ruffled his hair and put my arm around his shoulder. "We will, too. It'll just take time."

Evan cleared his throat and nodded. When he looked over my shoulder, his eyes widened slightly. "Come on. Breakfast is going to get cold."

He put his hand on my back and practically pushed me down the stairs. As we descended, I had half a second to turn around to see what in the world my brother had looked at. There was nothing there.

※

"I thought you got bread."

My mom and dad were already in the kitchen when we came in. The kitchen wasn't as outdated as the rest of the house, surprisingly. Apparently, it had been newly renovated right before Old Man Mosley died twenty years ago, and the appliances were like new—well new in nineteen ninety-nine.

The walls were a bright but muted yellow. The cabinets were white. A farmhouse sink sat under a boarded-up window. The stainless-steel stove hadn't lasted the last two decades without getting grimy, but it still worked, as evidenced by the bacon sizzling in an iron pan. A little white table, the one from our old home, thank goodness, sat in a breakfast nook to the side of the kitchen. Enough chairs for all of us, plus an extra unmatching wooden one for when Bradley came over— if he ever came over again.

"I did get bread," Mama answered my dad, rummaging through the bags of groceries they'd brought from our old house.

"Apparently, you didn't. How am I supposed to have a bacon sandwich without bread?"

Evan and I stopped in our tracks and looked at each other. My parents had always been sickeningly sweet to each other. I can't remember the last time they argued. I'm sure they did. Nobody's parents are perfect, but if mine did fight, they never did in front of us.

In fact, this little tiff was the first time I'd ever seen them have any sort of disagreement. Stress from the new house, maybe?

"Be thankful I got up and cooked you bacon," Mama countered.

"Lot of good it does without bread," my dad answered back curtly.

Okay … Evan and I grabbed our backpacks, even though we probably wouldn't need them for the day. It was the last day, after all.

"I'm taking Evan to school," I called.

"Have a good day." Mama had a fake happiness to her voice.

"We will. You, too," I called as the door slammed behind us. "What was that about?" I asked Evan.

"Apparently bread ... and bacon," Evan answered as he grabbed his bike.

I liked school, but I found myself desperate to be there. I hadn't been in the house a full day yet, and I was already tired of hearing about it. At least at school, no one would mention it. I could have my last day in peace.

A big smile pulled on my lips when we rounded the corner of the house; Bradley sat there on his bike, waiting for us. He kept his eyes on me, not allowing them to wander toward the house.

"Good to see you," I said. I would have run up and hugged him if he liked hugs.

"Good to see you, too. Ready?"

I was. The three of us rode down the sidewalk and away from Mosley Manor, a place I was thankful I didn't have to think about for the next eight hours.

CHAPTER SIX

"OH—my—GOSH! You live in Mosley Manor!" Gracie Redding nearly knocked me over as she grabbed onto my shoulder and didn't let go. Oh, she wasn't the first person to ask me about Mosley Manor since I'd been at school. Only like the twenty-first. So much for running away from it.

"It's nothing," Bradley answered for me like a good best friend would. Gracie was all right … now. Back in fourth grade, she was horrible to me. Made fun of me. She made my fourth-grade year miserable. Ever since sixth grade, though, for some reason, Gracie had talked to me like a human being. I wasn't sure what to think about it. I always expected the other shoe to drop when it came to her, like this entire year had been a setup for something—I just wasn't sure what yet.

"Nothing?" Gracie stopped in front of us, making us stop, too. (It was either that or fall right over her. I didn't particularly want to fall over her.)

"Excuse us, Gracie. We have to get to class." And we did. In about fifteen minutes. The late bell hadn't rung yet, but that wasn't important.

She held up her manicured hand to stop us. Her nails

were painted bubblegum pink, and they were long enough to be weapons. "You can't get away from me that quickly." She gave the fakest giggle of all time. "I want to know the details. How's the house? Did you see any ghosts? Does Old Man Mosley really walk around and eat children?"

"Yes," I deadpanned, staring her right in her perfect blue eyes.

She frowned. "Yes? Yes, what?"

"Yes, I saw Old Man Mosley. Where do you think Evan is today?"

She stepped back ever so slightly, then crossed her arms. "You think I'm stupid, don't you, Ava Kirkland."

It was better than Dorkland. "No, I don't. I'm just tired of people asking so many questions about my house. It's a house. There's a floor and ceilings and walls."

"And mice," Bradley added, not so helpfully. Mice were better than ghosts.

Gracie's face contorted. "Mice. *Ick*. Okay, well, once you get the vermin problem under control, you need to have me over. I'd love to spend the night."

"Yeah, maybe," I said so we could leave.

"Next weekend, then. I'll tell my parents."

"I'll ask mine," I said pointedly. If I ever told my parents I was doing anything before asking them, it would be the last thing I ever did.

Gracie moved to the side, letting Bradley and me pass.

We were out of earshot when Bradley bent down and said, "What was that about? You're going to let Gracie stay with you?"

I shrugged. "It's not a big deal."

He tilted his head like he didn't believe me.

"It's not. I promise. And hey" —I lightly nudged him with my elbow— "think about it this way. If Gracie comes over, maybe Old Man Mosley will eat her."

I meant it as a joke. Bradley seemed to consider the possibility.

The rest of the day wasn't any better. A thunderstorm, one the weatherman hadn't predicted, popped up over the school. It rained so hard and so fast that the dodgeball tournament had to be moved into the gym, which would have been fine, except lightning struck a tree near the building, sending limbs and debris through the ceiling and ruining the floor.

So much for a grand day. No end-of-the-year dodgeball tournament, and no gym to kill time in. We ended up back in our classes, movie on, and the entire class leaning over and asking me about Mosley Manor. As much as I had loved talking about it before, it was getting old really fast.

At lunch, it seemed my little brother had a similar problem. He found me, like he sometimes did, keeping his tray in his hands. He knew better than to sit with me, but he leaned down and asked, "Is everyone obsessed with our house?"

I nodded and tore off a bite of my ham sandwich.

"They'll never understand," he said, a hint of sadness in his voice as he went and sat alone. That wasn't like him. Normally, he found a group of friends to sit with. What was with him?

By the time the three o'clock bell rang, the weather had cleared up, and Bradley was already at his bike. "Come on, slowpoke."

"Not all of us are as excited to get away from school as you are." A snail passed me, I feel like pointing out.

"You aren't avoiding your house, are you?"

"No."

"The one you aren't afraid of."

"No."

"The one you invited Gracie to."

"To be eaten in," I reminded him.

He kicked the stand up on his bike. I'd love to kick the grin off his face. "Wanna go the long way home?" he asked, as he did every afternoon. And every afternoon, I'd tell him no, that it would be quicker to go past Mosley Manor. In anticipation of my response, Bradley already had his bike turned east.

"Yes," I answered, surprising both him and me.

He turned toward me and raised a brow. "Yes?"

"I mean, you asked. Let's take the long way home. We can make a circle, drop you off first since I know what my house does to you, then I can ride the rest of the way by myself."

"You sure? I was just kidding."

"I know, but to be honest, some time away from that place would do me good."

He opened his mouth to say something.

"In a scientific way, of course."

"Of course." Without another word, like the good friend he is, he turned his bike north, and we disappeared on Fifth Avenue. If we took enough time, his mom would be home when we got there. Maybe she'd invite me in. Maybe she'd invite me to stay for supper. Maybe we could all watch a movie together. Maybe it would be nearly dark before I had to go back to Mosley Manor—to home.

Maybe I could finally get a break from it.

CHAPTER SEVEN

As per the theme of the day, Bradley's mom wasn't at home when we got there. Kayla's car sat in the driveway. Kayla was the eighteen-year-old who came over to watch him until his mom got off. Bradley hated having a "babysitter." He was twelve years old after all and, in his mind, could stay by himself. The state of Tennessee didn't feel the same—at least that's what his mom told him. Kayla started staying with him when she was sixteen, and he was ten. She was saving for college and had been accepted to Tennessee Tech University. She was excited. Bradley was really excited. He hoped his mom didn't try to replace Kayla.

"Guess this is my stop." Bradley sounded sad. I felt sad.

"Yeah. Looks like it. Have fun with Kayla." I smirked because I knew he wouldn't have fun.

"She'll be on the phone with her boyfriend the entire time. My mom pays her twenty dollars an hour to do nothing."

"Not nothing," I corrected. "She watches and protects you. Twenty dollars is well worth the price to protect you."

He nudged me back, probably a bit of payback from when

I hit him earlier. "I'll send her to your house, then. Protect you from big bad mice and kid-eating ghosts."

I didn't know why it happened, but I flinched when he said it, and a chill ran up my spine. I plastered on a huge smile to hide it and looked down the street, accepting my fate.

"Hey, do you want to come in and watch a movie? I know Kayla won't mind. It'll keep me out of her hair for a few hours. Unless you are super excited to get back to your mice and paranormal phenomenon."

"There's no paranormal phenomenon. I'm just tired of everyone treating my new house like it's something special. It's not." I pointed to our old house next to Bradley's. "That one was special. The new one is just … old." This, I said way too strongly.

I looked down the road at all the nice houses, pretty, full-grown trees, flowers, happiness—life. I sincerely didn't want to go home.

"I mean, I don't mind going home, but if you want me to keep you company from Kayla, I'll do you a favor and stay for a movie."

He smirked. "Yes, I need you to do me a favor and watch a movie with me."

"Only because you want me to.

"I understand." He smiled and shook his head.

He was a good friend.

We went inside, just as normal. Grabbing some snacks, we went into the den to watch a movie. Bradley wanted to watch *Coraline*. After I glared at him, we settled on our favorite anime that we'd already watched thirteen times, not that we cared.

Once we'd binged six episodes, I stretched and knew I had to face my fate. "I'd better get before it gets too dark."

Normally, at this time, he would say something like, "See

you tomorrow," or "Have a good weekend," even though we hadn't gone more than a day without seeing each other since we were six. Living next door to each other would do that. But with me living down the street, what was there to say?

"I'll swing by tomorrow," he promised.

"You don't have to. I know that house freaks you out." It made me sad to think it, though. I wanted my best friend to feel comfortable coming over whenever he wanted. Eventually, we'd get it fixed up, and he wouldn't be scared of it. It would be Kirkland Manor instead of Mosley Manor, not that it had as good of a ring to it.

"I'll be there. We can go to the pool or something."

"Or something," I agreed. I waved to Kayla as I left the house, grabbed my bike, and pedaled away. Before I was out of his driveway, I noticed Bradley standing on his porch. I put on my brakes and turned toward him. "Thank you."

"For what?"

"For everything." And that encompassed a lot. "Thanks for facing your fears for me."

"I wouldn't chance being eaten for anyone else in the world." He laughed with a wink.

I rolled my eyes but secretly appreciated the gesture. I rode home just as the streetlights came on and began to hum. I'd put it off long enough.

Time to go home.

CHAPTER EIGHT

The house was lit up when I got there. My parents had been busy all day, pulling the wood off of the windows, mowing the hayfield of the yard, changing light bulbs. In the dim light of the neighborhood, Mosley Manor looked like an old woman's birthday cake, full of light and candles.

Mosley Manor. I had to stop thinking of it as that.

This was my house ... MINE. My family's. It was time for me to get used to that.

Evan's bike was propped up next to the fence. I put mine next to it and had to smile. His bike had his favorite superhero on it. He'd long-since outgrown the character, but his legs hadn't. My parents wouldn't get him a new bike until he got tall enough to outgrow this one. He took that as a warning ... never get a bike based on who you like at the moment. Cause then you are stuck with it.

I threw my backpack on my shoulder and headed up the porch steps and into the house. The front door hung wide open, held in place by an old chair that had probably been last painted in the fifties, based on how the green paint peeled and chipped.

I looked around the foyer, examining what all my parents had done and what sort of things they would want me to do. It was lucky for them that we bought this house during summer break. Evan and I would be here to help fix it up. Sneaky people.

The off-white wallpaper with the ornate gold design still hung in place. I had to admit, the history buff in me really wanted to keep it there. It was historically accurate, not in bad shape, and honestly, really pretty. Probably the prettiest thing in the house so far. I liked it, as much as I hated to admit I liked anything in this house.

I sincerely needed to get over that way of thinking. The house wasn't bad. It had good bones, as they said on the renovation shows my mom watched. The ghost stories would die down (no pun intended) when we moved in and made it pretty. That's all the house needed—a family to love it.

Besides Old Man Mosley, I wondered who had lived in the house. It had to be over a hundred years old. Lots of families had to have lived there—children, husbands, wives, dogs … cats … I was sure these walls had seen laughter and, unfortunately, pain. No telling the stories they could tell or the things they'd seen.

If only walls could talk, as they said.

Not really sure who "they" were, but they seemed to say a lot of wise things.

Not sure where to put my backpack, I slid it next to Evan's to the right of the front door. We would move them tomorrow probably. Mama liked for us to keep all of our backpacks from school. I'm sure there was a box of them somewhere that needed to be put away.

"Hello?" I asked the wind.

There was no one else around to answer. That wasn't like my mom, especially on the last day of school. Normally, she plopped me down in the living room and asked me a thousand questions about my grades, my friends, my summer plans—which always included Bradley. When I finally had something interesting to tell her, she wasn't around. I took that as a sign that I shouldn't ask her if Gracie Redding could come to the house and spend the night. The only reason she wanted to come was for the ghosts. The fact that there weren't any would make her underwhelmed. Course then she'd start the rumor that there were, in fact, no ghosts in Mosley Manor and people would finally leave me alone about living in the town haunted house.

Maybe inviting her over would be a good thing.

"Mama?" I headed for the kitchen. My stomach had the rumblies, and I needed some sort of snack before supper. Sure enough, Mama sat at the kitchen table, a spread of papers laid in front of her, and judging by the way her head fell on her hand and the way the vein in her forehead pulsed, she was stressed.

Perhaps homeownership wasn't the dream she'd bargained for. Maybe it was a nightmare.

"Mama? You okay?"

With a jump, she looked up from her papers, her eyes red and puffy. "Hi, yeah, hi, Ava. Sorry, I didn't hear you come in." She sat up and put on a fake smile. At least it looked fake to me. "How was the last day of sixth grade?"

I pulled out a chair and sat down. "It was okay, I guess. I made straight As." I had been pretty proud of that since I had a teacher who graded incredibly strict. I wasn't sure I'd make it in the beta club, but thankfully, I worked hard enough. My teacher said she was proud of me. I couldn't help but be proud of me, too.

"That's great, baby!" Mama still called me baby. I didn't mind as long as it wasn't around Bradley or any other friend I might have over.

Speaking of … "Okay, you can totally say no, but I have

this friend, Gracie. I mean, she's not really a friend, more of an acquaintance." More like a person who made my fourth-grade year horrible, but who's counting?

"You mean you talk to other children besides Bradley?" she said with a wink.

"Haha," I deadpanned. "I talk to other people; I just don't like them as much as I like him."

Mama's brows rose.

"Not like that, Mama. Glory! You are turning into the people at school." Maybe asking her was a bad idea.

"I know. I'm sorry. I just think it's really sweet, the friendship you and Bradley have. A lot of people don't even like the person they marry that much." She said the last part so sadly that it caught my attention.

"You and Daddy are best friends." It wasn't even a question. It was a statement.

She hesitated before smiling so big I thought her lips would burst. "Yes, baby. Yes, we are." She patted me on the hand a little extra to get her point across. *Okaaay* ... "So, what were you wanting to ask me?"

"Gracie Redding. She wanted to know if she could come over to the house sometime this summer and spend the night. She's convinced it's haunted or something, and she wants to document her experiences."

"Everyone and that ridiculous haunting story." Mama scoffed. "You don't believe it, do you?"

"Me? No. I don't. I think we need a lot of mouse traps, but not haunted. It might be telling if she saw it for herself. She'll tell some of her other friends, and they'll stop asking me what it's like living in Mosley Manor, or how many ghosts I've seen, or look at me like I'm crazy because I live here." I hadn't meant to let that last little statement come out, but once it had, I looked at Mama. She bit her lip like she hadn't considered what the move would do to Evan and me at school.

"You need to not care what others think or say."

"I know … I know … but like, if she could see there isn't anything here, maybe it would stop the rumors … from hurting … Evan." Had Evan been affected by the rumors like I had? Who knew? I hadn't talked to him today. He had baseball practice after school, and Mama's friend, Jean, who had a son Evan's age, had taken him.

"Evan is being teased at school?"

"I'm not sure … I … okay. Bad idea. Sorry I asked." I stood up, ready to disappear into my room and never come out.

"She can come over," Mama said, surprising me.

"She can?"

Mama nodded. "Give us a week or two to get the house more livable. We are getting started on the bathroom tomorrow. Once that's finished, your friend, Gracie, is it, can come over."

I didn't know whether to be happy or sad by the news. "You sure?" I gave her a second to back out.

"I'm sure. It will be nice to have people in the house. It seems so sad. Like it used to host grand parties, and now it's a shell of its former self."

I hadn't thought of it that way. "Okay, thanks. I'll call her tomorrow and let her know."

Mama nodded, her eyes already back on the pile of papers in front of her. "Your father went to get takeout for supper. He will be home soon. In the meantime, can you do me a favor?"

"Sure."

"I put the box with your old school things in it, backpacks and such, up in the attic this morning. Can you take yours and Evan's up there now, so we don't lose them?"

My body froze for a second, and words wouldn't form. "You want me … to go up … into the attic … alone?"

She tilted her head at me like I had five eyes. "Thought you weren't afraid of ghosts."

"I'm not." I kinda lied. Attics were creepy. "I'm afraid of spiders."

CHAPTER NINE

E van's backpack was much heavier than mine. What all did they do in fourth grade? Mine for gold? Bring all the rocks home?

Part of me wanted to go through his backpack and toss a lot of the things I knew Mama would never miss. Another part of me felt guilty for thinking that. Mama had her reasons for wanting our things, whatever they were, and if it meant I had to trek up the steps and put them in the attic, then so be it.

The thought of the attic made me shudder.

It was only for the potential spiders.

Only.

For.

The.

Spiders.

With one backpack on each shoulder, I made my way up the stairs to the second floor. My bedroom door was open as per usual. The bathroom door was closed, again, as per usual. Funny how we hadn't been in this house long, and there were already 'usuals.'

My brother's bedroom door was cracked open slightly. Light flooded through the dark hallway, and it hit me that I hoped the attic had electricity, because it would be awfully dark without it.

I needed a flashlight, just in case.

My brother usually had a few laying around. People liked to give them to him as gifts for birthdays and holidays. In my experience, people didn't know how to buy for a boy, not as easily as they could buy for me anyway. A flashlight was an easy and practical gift. I tended to get money. I was okay with that.

Except for when I needed a flashlight.

A little green floral runner started at the bedroom at the far end of the hallway, ran down the middle of the hall, and continued down to the bottom of the staircase. It had seen better days. The fabric was frayed at the edges, and the color was bright in some places and muted where any drop of sun landed over the years. It also acted as a sound barrier. The hardwood underneath, when stepped on directly, caused a loud pop with each footstep. It sounded like those ghost footsteps on those ghost shows I didn't watch … but totally did.

My footsteps didn't make a sound as I crept toward Evan's room. The closer I got, the more I heard what sounded like Evan talking. At first, I thought he had company or something. A few times, he'd had his friend come over after baseball practice. Evan was talking. There would be silence … then Evan would talk again. He didn't sound angry, just agitated.

I inched closer, listening. I wasn't one to eavesdrop on my little brother, but if it had something important to do with me or some sort of information I needed to know, then I most certainly would listen—for his own good, of course.

It was the most bizarre conversation I'd ever heard.

I'd heard people talking to themselves before. It's pretty

common. What I'd never witnessed was someone saying something, then nothing … then nothing.

I leaned in to listen closer. It was only Evan's voice, but there was most certainly a pause after he spoke.

"Yeah, summer's okay."

Pause.

"I like summer. Or I did. Not sure how I'll like it here."

"I'm not being mean. I'm just saying … it's kinda creepy."

"Not you …"

The floor creaked, thanks to my big foot, and I heard a scramble in Evan's room, followed by the door opening just a little bit wider. "Ava, what are you doing here?"

"I live here, remember." How could either of us forget?

"I mean, what are you doing next to my room? You can't come in."

"Nothing would bother me worse. Who are you talking to?" I peeked inside, but just as soon as I thought I recognized a shadow of a person, it disappeared.

"Nobody." Evan slammed his body in between the door-frame and the door so that I couldn't see in. Nope, he wasn't acting weird at all.

"Nobody, huh? You just decide to talk to yourself."

His face turned red. He opened his mouth to say something, then something behind him must have caught his attention, because he turned his head toward the left, acted like he was listening to something, then focused back on me. "What I do is none of your business. I do appreciate your concern, but I'm fine."

I wasn't going to let it go that easily. "I think you're talking to someone."

His face got redder, and he squirmed just a bit. "Who? A ghost?"

I scoffed, nearly dropping our backpacks. "No. Something real. Like maybe an imaginary friend."

"That's it!" He snapped his fingers so fast I was surprised I saw it.

"What's it?"

"An imaginary friend! I have an imaginary friend that only I can see and hear and talk to. His name is David. Ow!" Evan grunted and rubbed the back of his shoulder.

"What?" I asked.

"Nothing."

"Nothing?"

"Nope." He smiled much too broadly. "Nothing at all."

"Interesting." I didn't know what to make of his strange behavior. I supposed we all got lonely sometimes and had to make up people to talk to. In fact, I remembered doing it a few times during fourth grade when Gracie was mean to me. And now she was coming over to spend the night at my house. My cheeks would hurt from all the fake smiling I would have to do.

"Why are you here, anyway?" Evan shifted from foot to foot. He was ready to get rid of me. These backpacks were heavy. Despite how weird he was being, I was ready to get rid of him, too.

"Oh, I need your flashlight. Mama wants me to take these in the attic where the rest of them are. I was afraid there weren't any lights up there."

"So, you wanted one of mine."

"That was the idea. Have you unpacked them yet? I promise I'll bring it back on my way down to supper."

Evan hesitated. His eyes scanned the hallway until they got to the door at the far end of the hallway. From what I recalled about my trip through the house last night, behind those doors were steps leading to the attic, a place I never wanted to go—especially this early in our stay.

"Yeah, hold on a second."

Evan said something else I couldn't understand. Finally,

he stuck out his hand with a green and black mini flashlight. "Here. Keep it. I don't want it back."

"Sure?"

He nodded like he was tired. He couldn't have been that tired. He was used to staying up very late at our old house. "I'm sure."

I started to say thank you when the door slammed in my face. How very rude of him.

Whispers crept from behind the door, whispers so low, I couldn't make out what they were saying. Sounded angry, though.

Okay then …

I took our backpacks and the flashlight toward the attic steps. The plan was to get in, get out, go downstairs to eat, then go to my room and relax for the rest of the night.

First, I'd have to put my mattress and my own sheets on the bed so I wouldn't have to smell the decade-old dirt, which had piled up and assaulted me the previous nights. We really should have moved in the sleeping things first. It would have been smart.

I closed my eyes with my hand on the doorknob. Why did I feel so nervous? It was a room in a house. Nothing more. Nothing less. My rational mind told me to get over it and go up the steps. My irrational part was afraid Old Man Mosley's skeleton would fall out of the door when I opened it.

Rational person that I was, I quickly opened the door … and jumped back, just in case any spiders or snakes … or Old Man Mosley fell on top of my head. Thankfully, nothing happened, just as I knew it wouldn't.

With a laugh at myself, I flipped on the flashlight and started up the creaking steps.

The steps were much steeper than ones from the first floor to the second. I'd seen pictures of the Winchester Mystery House at school. My teacher was into spooky things, and occasionally, she'd find a reason to show us supposedly haunted places in history class. I didn't mind. Not that I believed the house was haunted, but I loved the architecture and history.

Anyway, the house had been built by Mary Winchester. She was the widow of the man who invented Winchester guns. After his death, she felt guilty for all the lives her husband's guns had taken and felt like her bad luck connected to it. So, to keep the spirits of the people who had died from the guns away, Mary bought a farmhouse in California and began renovating it.

For the next forty years, the work never stopped. She built doors that led to walls, windows in floors, stairs to nowhere, to name a few of the house's oddities. I assumed that ghosts could just go through walls no matter if there was a door to nowhere or not—if there were ghosts … which there weren't.

The point was, the stairs to the attic reminded me of the picture Mrs. Fallon had shown us of the 'stairs to nowhere' in the Winchester Mystery House; narrow, steep, dark. Hopefully, these stairs led to a room and not an end.

I shined my flashlight up higher and noticed rafters above me. So yeah, attic.

Attics meant spiders, and, *shivers*, bats in some cases. The thought sent a chill down my spine. I'd rather see a ghost than a bat. I had my limits.

Once my head was higher than the floor, I used the flashlight to examine the room. The light disappeared before it reached the corners of the room, so that told me it was fairly big. I took another step up and shined the light on the floor. I hoped it was sturdy. I didn't want to fall through the floor and land in the bathtub or something. It seemed pretty sturdy. At least it was solid.

In front of me, pushed against the wall, was something tall and thin, pressed so far against the wall that the light from my flashlight could barely reach it. It was covered with a white sheet, and if I had been Bradley, I would have run, thinking it was a ghost.

My heart had skipped a beat for a second, just a second, though. I hadn't been expecting it. All the other things my mom had brought up there weren't covered with white sheets. There were several plastic totes, a few boxes, a chest that my mom had since she was a girl, and one large box that I knew contained our Christmas tree.

The steps moaned with each step I took. The smell hit me like a limb to the nose: musty, moldy, like an old gas station bathroom that had been kept fairly okay, but with a smell that nearly knocked you down. That was mold. That was icky.

I needed to get in and out before this stuff got in my lungs and made me cough all summer.

After I climbed the last two steps, I stood straight up, finally in the attic. It wasn't so bad. I'd made it. Just had to find the box, put in the backpacks, and leave. No big deal.

Just to make myself feel better, I bounced on the floor-boards ever so slightly to make sure they could hold up the weight. They seemed pretty sturdy. Thank goodness.

I shined the light to my left on the first set of totes. Baby pictures, baby clothes, baby toys—my mom had a thing about keeping our baby things. Evan thought it was because she wanted another baby. I tried not to think about it.

The next section of totes was labeled plates, Grandma's china set, old records.

I ran the light over, careful not to shine it at the rafters and awaken any rodent that might be in there. More totes, a few boxes, the mirror with the cover gone … more totes.

Wait …

I shined the flashlight back. The tall thing in the back of the attic, the one against the wall that I could barely see before … the white cover hung gingerly over one side.

When had it moved?

Had it moved?

Had it been that way the entire time, and I'd simply seen it wrong?

In any case, my heart sped up, and I decided it was time to get out of this attic. Quickly, I looked to the right and found the tote that said BACKPACKS. Forgetting my fear of the floor, I hurried over and threw up the lid. I threw our backpacks in it, tossed the lid back on top, and forced it down. It took a few shoves since the tote was pretty full, but I didn't care. The sound of scraping behind me caused the hair on the back of my neck to rise. I froze, listening, barely breathing so I could hear the sound again.

One second.

Two seconds …

Nothing happened …

I'd always heard people had a fight or flight response. I most certainly believed that. My body wanted flight. Getting it to move was the difficult part.

It was just a noise … just a noise … a simple scrape in an old house … Truthfully, I felt pretty silly—I, who wasn't afraid of anything, was letting this attic get the better of me.

I pushed down on the tote one last time, and the edges snapped into place. Thank goodness, because I hadn't intended to try again.

I turned to leave and screamed.

CHAPTER TEN

The white sheet had fallen off of the mirror, somehow, and I had been met by my reflection, staring back at me. At first, I thought I was a ghost, which made me scream. Then, when I got my wits about me and realized that I didn't believe in ghosts, I actually focused and, yup, there I was, with my blonde ringlet hair and blue eyes, same as ever.

I wasn't sure how the white sheet fell or why, and I knew I didn't care. With my task completed, there was no reason for me to stay up there any longer than I had to. That mirror could reflect the darkness for all I cared.

Without waiting another second, I turned my flashlight toward the stairs and heard the worst sound I'd ever heard in my life. Literally, or figuratively I suppose, my heart stopped. Every muscle in my body froze. I stopped breathing. Even with my body freaking out, my mind raced.

I knew what had made that sound even before I forced my flashlight to shine down: the door to the attic had shut.

Evan.

He had to have done it.

When we were younger, he liked to play tricks on me.

Nothing dangerous or really scary, except the one time he put the plastic spider on the towel before I got out of the shower. That had been the worst one by far—until this.

I was more scared of what the closed door meant than whether there was anything up in the attic with me—or if something paranormal had closed the door. Because I knew, in my brain, that nothing else had closed the door. It had been Evan. Simple as that.

Once I made my muscles move again, I stomped down the steps so hard my footsteps echoed through the vast attic. "Evan Kirkland! I'm going to get you!" I pushed the door just as I turned the knob.

It didn't budge.

What? No … no.

"Evan Scott Kirkland!" I knocked against the door. "If you're trying to scare me, it's not going to work! Open the door!"

Nothing. Not even a rustle on the other side.

I leaned my ear against the wood, listening for any kind of footsteps, breathing, or movement to give Evan away.

If I didn't know any better, I'd say he wasn't anywhere to be found.

So why was the door locked?

Holding the flashlight in my mouth, I twisted the knob while pushing on the door. It had to open. It wasn't locked when I came into the attic. The knob didn't feel like it had a key lock, and even if it did, who would have a door in the attic that would keep someone locked in?

"Evan!" I banged against the door, adrenaline pumping through my veins.

I knew he closed it. He had to. He probably slammed it and ran away. Didn't explain why it wouldn't open, but that was neither here nor there.

I banged harder, so hard my knuckles hurt. "Evan! Open

this door now!"

I shined the light at the doorknob, trying to see if there was any way to pry it open. The knob was old and brassy with a smooth round finish and no indication of a keyhole, not that there would be. Who would put a lock inside an attic?

I shined the light up the door to see how stable it was. Maybe, if I was lucky, I could slam against it like those people in the movies do, and it would pop open.

Little lines, no bigger than the edge of a pencil, were carved in the wood—lots of lines. Intrigued, I looked closer. There were so many. What made them?

I ran my fingertips over a few of them, careful not to slide my fingernail under them. I didn't want to get splinters from the wood under my …

Fingernails.

I stepped back and placed my hand over my mouth. My eyes were wide, and I couldn't look away.

Fingernails.

The cuts and lines in the door were scratched by fingernails!

My mind raced.

Someone had been locked in this room.

Locked like me.

They couldn't get out.

They probably beat on the door. Begged someone to get them out.

And then, resorted to clawing at the door to get it to open.

"What happened to you?" I gasped, slowly reaching out to touch my fingers to the scratches. I couldn't imagine doing something so horrible.

"Mama, please!" I screamed as hard as I could. I didn't want to be up here any longer. If Evan couldn't hear me, maybe, just maybe, Mama could. I beat on the door, jiggled the handle, everything, anything to get anyone's attention.

"Mama, help!" I pounded the door until my knuckles hurt.

Until blood dripped from my fingers.

No one came. No one heard me.

Exhausted.

Terrified.

My flashlight flickered as I headed back up the steps. Maybe there was a vent or something I could yell down. A window I could break. Something.

I hit the flashlight against my hand, willing it not to die on me.

When I got to the top of the stairs, the white sheet was back over the mirror.

Our backpacks were still on my shoulders.

My …

"Ava Anne Kirkland, what's taking you so long?" Mama's nearby voice made me jump. I dropped the backpacks and turned toward the door. I'd never been so happy to see someone in my life.

"Mama!" I ran down and gave her a big hug.

She didn't hug me back. "Ava, I asked you to put the backpacks away, not disappear."

"I didn't. I mean, I did. I put them back."

She looked around me and eyed the pile of them on the floor. It didn't make any sense to me, either. "And I tried to get out, but the door is closed."

Mama's brow rose before she used her thumb to point to the door behind her. The very open door. "This door?"

"Yes, that door. It was closed. Locked."

"Ava, this door was open when I found you. You were just standing there with the backpacks on your shoulders, not moving."

That made no sense. "No, Mama. It was closed. I tried to get you to hear me. See, I bruised and bloodied my knuckles knocking." I showed my hands to her.

Instead of being horrified, she huffed. "Ava, do you think this is funny?"

What? "No, not one bit. I don't think it's in the least bit funny to be locked in a room and unable to get out. I don't think bleeding is funny." I pushed my hands out to her again.

She turned them toward me so I could see. "There's no blood, Ava."

"Yes, there is. You just aren't looking."

I shoved them back in her face again. I knew what I'd seen. I knew what I'd done.

"Ava, stop this. I know you aren't happy about the move, but pretending like this is dangerous. Now, come with me, I have someone to introduce you to."

Mama left the room. When she did, the lights from the hallway flooded where I stood on the staircase. I looked down at my hands and nothing ... no blood. No bruises.

"What in the world ...?" I whispered, turning my hands over and over. "Evan," I told Mama. "Evan locked me in." I didn't have as much conviction in my voice this time.

In a huff, Mama spun on her heel and glared at me. "Evan has been with me for the last hour, Ava. He came downstairs right after you went up. He didn't lock you anywhere, and, to be factual, you weren't even locked in! Now, stop with this charade and come downstairs with me. Now."

Without waiting for a reply, she spun back on her heel and disappeared down the stairs.

All alone on the second floor, I looked at my hands one last time. There was nothing there. I turned and looked at the door, still open. Fingernail marks were still etched in the wood.

What in the world was happening?

CHAPTER ELEVEN

E van's door was closed when I went by it. I wanted to barge inside to see what the little bugger had been up to, but I held myself back. Mama said he had been downstairs with her this entire time. I supposed he had, but still … something weird was going on in there. Course, I knew my brother. That might be par for the course with him.

Muffled voices came from the kitchen. Curious, I wondered who in the world would be here this time of night. The only people who ever came to our old house was Bradley and occasionally his mom. Maybe that's who it was? Maybe his mom had gotten home, and they'd come over to see our new house.

Renewed with hope, I bounced down the rest of the stairs and didn't stop until I rounded the corner through the living room and straight into the kitchen behind my mama.

Then I saw who it was.

And my joy faded.

Gracie Redding.

And some lady who looked like she should work at the jewelry counter at some fancy diamond store.

"Ava!" Gracie squealed and ran toward me. She hugged me so tightly I couldn't breathe. I glanced over to Mama for help, but she simply slumped against the wall with her arms crossed and frustration pouring out of her eyes, not literally. That would have been weird. "It's so good to see you!"

"Gracie," I could barely whisper. She had a death grip on me. "I just saw you at school today. Like six hours ago."

"I know." She finally let me go. "But it's been too long."

Behind her, Gracie's mama beamed with her hands clasped in front of her chest like she was so proud of her daughter for being nice to the little people. I was the little people in the scenario.

"Gracie told her mother you said she could spend the night tonight." Mama's words were strained.

I gently pushed Gracie back so I could have a little bit of personal space again. "No, what I said was I'd ask tonight if you could, then you could come over in a few weeks when we had the house in better shape. Remember, I told you that, Mama." I didn't want her to think I was a big liar. Mama didn't have many pet peeves. A liar was one of them.

Mama, who thankfully seemed to believe me, turned her attention to Mrs. Redding, who simply shrugged. "Gracie said you told her you could come over tonight."

"I must have misunderstood." Gracie beamed with all sugar and spice and everything syrupy. "But since I'm here …"

"Yes," her mother added. "Since she's here …"

Gracie didn't look much like her mother. Gracie had dark hair. Her mom had blonde from a salon. Gracie's eyes were blue. Her mom's were green—I'd read once that only two percent of the world had green eyes. Her mom had on pink high heels.

Pink.

High.

Heels.

To each his own.

Gracie had changed since school, too. She had on tight black jeans, black Converse shoes, and a long-sleeved black shirt with little rhinestones on the front pocket in the shape of a cat. Her hair was pulled back in a high ponytail, and her eyes were smoky with black liner around them. She had gotten into the part of "paranormal investigator."

Mama looked at me. I looked at her. I really wanted her to say Gracie couldn't stay. I'd had enough going on, and all I wanted to do was eat supper, if Daddy ever got home with it, and go to bed. Sure, I had to fix my mattress and my comforter, but that was a small price to pay to close my eyes and forget all about the horrible day.

I'd try to figure out what happened in the attic another day. Ignoring it seemed the best option.

"I suppose ..." my mom started, betraying me. "I suppose you can both stay for supper. The house isn't ready for overnight guests, just yet, but we can sit and chat while Ava takes Gracie on a tour of the house."

You'd have thought Mama gave Gracie a billion dollars. She jumped up and down, squealed, and grabbed me by the arm. "OMG! I'm so excited! So excited!" She reached in the bag she had draped across her shoulder and pulled out a phone. "I'll take pictures. See if I can catch any ghosts."

"Gracie," her mother admonished.

"Sorry. I mean, um, take pictures of the lovely house."

She was totally there to take pictures of ghosts.

"Okay. Thanks. Mom." My words were strained, and by the 'I'm so sorry' look she gave me, I was sure she got my meaning.

"Come on!" Gracie grabbed my arm and yanked me out of the kitchen, blabbering on about how she hoped Old Man Mosley made an appearance. "Have you seen anything unusual yet? Have you heard anything? Moaning or chains rattling? Oh! Have you been down to the basement?"

I stopped; a devilishly mean idea crossed my mind. I decided not to bring it up. Gracie was on her best behavior. She hadn't done anything bad, and okay, people can change. I shouldn't bring up anything she'd done to me in the past. Obviously, she felt bad about everything she'd done and said. If she hadn't, she wouldn't have come over, right? A small, honest smile crossed my face. Maybe this wouldn't be too bad.

"Let's go, Dorkland. Show me the good stuff!"

Dorkland.

Her old nickname for me.

My heart dropped, and I felt like a complete moron for thinking Gracie could ever change.

She froze as soon as she said it and turned to me with wide eyes like she hadn't meant to let Dorkland slip. But the ease in which the word came out of her mouth let me know that it was something she often said, probably to her friends who likely laughed and still made fun of me behind my back, even if they had stopped saying it to my face.

"Actually" —I plastered on a smile like I hadn't noticed she called me the worst name ever— "we do have an attic."

CHAPTER TWELVE

At the mention of the attic, Gracie suddenly turned a little bit paler. "You have an attic? Seriously?"

"I do." I grinned as I pondered all the ways I could scare her up there, so she'd never try to come here again. My days of being her Dorkland were done.

I'd never felt the need for revenge before, never. Even in fourth grade when she'd been so mean to me. I figured she'd grow out of it, and if she didn't, her opinion of me didn't matter. I liked myself. I liked my curly hair and my crooked smile. I liked how I loved science and social studies. I loved how I'd rather have history books for Christmas than gadgets. Not that there was anything wrong with not liking any of those things. The point was, I liked myself, and honestly, I hadn't cared what Gracie Redding said about me in a very long time.

Except … when we stepped up on the second floor, and she called me Dorkland again.

It was like a red filter fell over my eyes, and anger pulsed through me. I wanted nothing more than to make Gracie leave the house, screaming and peeing her pants after I scared her to death in the attic. I'd take a picture of the pee running down her leg and post it everywhere at school. Then she'd know what it was like to be made fun of.

Wait …

What was I thinking?

I realized immediately that the thoughts weren't my normal ones. I got mad sometimes (I was human after all), but I couldn't remember the last time I got this angry. Shaking angry. It was almost like watching someone else, feeling someone else's anger, allowing someone else's frustration to run through me.

Almost without thinking, I walked past Gracie, my shoulder hitting hers as I led her toward the attic door. It was closed. Had I left it closed earlier? I didn't remember. I didn't care to remember.

If Gracie noticed my change in attitude, she didn't mention it. I heard her phone behind me, snapping away. "What's this?" She asked, pushing on a door.

"My room." I kept on walking.

"And this one?"

"Bathroom." I made it to the attic door and opened it. "Ready to go inside?" I crossed my arms and motioned for her to go on in.

She hesitated and had every right to. If she knew what I planned on doing to her, the thoughts that had crept in my mind, she would have run down the steps and not stopped until she got to her house. It was almost like watching her on a movie screen. It looked real, but it didn't feel real. Like someone else was controlling me, and I was just hanging back, watching.

"Is there a light in there?" Gracie put her foot on the first step. My hand tightened on the door handle, anticipating what I was going to do.

"Yeah, toward the top of the wall," I lied. There was no

light up there. She'd be in the dark with nothing but her cell phone.

Boo. Hoo.

"You coming?" she asked, pushing up to the second step.

"After you."

Once her foot was securely inside the attic, I smiled and slammed the door shut.

"Ava!" she yelled, alone, in the dark. "Ava, let me out."

I didn't answer. Didn't want to answer. I held the knob in my hand, her pounding on the door falling on deaf ears. I didn't want to let her out.

I didn't …

I shook my head. What was I doing? What in the world was I doing? Gracie might have deserved this, but I didn't want to be like her. I didn't want to stoop to her level. This wasn't me … it wasn't.

As quickly as I could, I pulled the door open, allowing the light from the hallway to engulf Gracie, who looked terrified.

I felt about the size of an ant.

"Do you think that's funny?" I could tell she was trying not to show how afraid she was. Gracie Redding had always prided herself on not being afraid of anything. I supposed Mosley Manor had been her ultimate test. By the way her eyes were huge, her breathing ragged, her phone grasped in her hands so tightly her fingertips were white, yeah, she was scared, and I felt horrible about it.

"Let me go get a flashlight. Sometimes the light doesn't work in here." I turned on my heel and headed to Evan's room. The one he let me borrow earlier was downstairs, and I had no intention of going all the way back down there to get it.

Before I got to his room, the attic door slammed shut without me anywhere near it.

"Ava!" Gracie screamed in full terror, making the hairs on my arms stand up.

I ran to the door, but the knob wouldn't budge.

I knew I hadn't done it this time.

CHAPTER THIRTEEN

I ran toward the door, my heart pounding in my ears. I hadn't done it that time. I didn't think she'd done it to herself. There had to be another logical explanation for why the door slammed shut, but it would have to wait for another time to figure it out.

"Ava! Please! I'm sorry. I'm so sorry!" More pounding on the door. "Ava, I …"

Her words cut out.

As did the pounding.

I slid to a stop. For a second, I hesitated. Irrational terror, that's what they called it in a book I read once. Irrational terror was what Bradley had of this house. There was nothing here that could hurt him. There was nothing here that could hurt me. Gracie was safe.

But somewhere deep down, I knew that hypothesis was wrong. Something was in the house. Something did have Gracie.

Something was behind the door, and that something wasn't nice.

"Gracie?" I whispered like she could hear me through the

door with a whisper. I let out a deep breath and pulled in every bit of nerves I had. With my hand trembling, I reached out and touched the door. Once my fingers touched the wood, I jumped back like I thought it would bite me or something. "Stop letting this house get to you," I ordered myself.

Feeling a bit more confident, I put my hand on the knob and started to twist. Like before, it wouldn't budge.

I knew what Gracie was going through, how she felt stuck in there. Was my time in there real or some elaborate daydream? I couldn't be sure. What I was sure of was I didn't want her to go through the same terror I had.

"Gracie! Talk to me!" I banged on the door, hoping it wouldn't scare her more.

When she didn't answer me, it was me that became more scared. "Gracie! I'm going to get help, okay? I'm going to get Mama." I turned to leave, hoping she would be okay until I got back.

"Mama can't help me."

It caught me off guard. The voice didn't sound like Gracie's. I mean, it did … It had to. It was more … I don't know … nasally, with more of a Southern twang like mine. Gracie grew up in Nashville, and her drawl wasn't as thick as mine.

If I didn't know better, and I did know better, I would think there was someone else in that room with Gracie.

But there couldn't be.

It had to be Gracie's voice.

"Yes, she can," I answered Gracie because it had to be Gracie. "Hold on. I'll be right back!"

Before I got to the stairs, a bellowing scream erupted through the hallway. The pitch was so shrill I covered my ears. Even my brother peaked out of his room to see what it was.

I had to decide what to do quickly. I couldn't leave Gracie

in there any longer than I already had. I was so mad at myself for even putting her in that situation to begin with, but I couldn't dwell on that now. I had to get her out.

I grabbed Evan by the shoulders and spun him toward me, his big eyes in some sort of confused shock. "Run downstairs and get Mama and Mrs. Redding."

"Mrs. Who?"

"Just do it! Tell them Gracie is in trouble, and we need them now."

He didn't budge.

"Go!" I nearly dragged him out of his room and pushed him down the first step. Not very kind, but I didn't feel the kindest in my life, either. The rage that had filled me earlier had gone—mostly—but had left me with a sick feeling in my stomach.

Why weren't Mama and Mrs. Redding already running up the stairs to save Gracie? They had to have heard the screaming. People on Mars had to have heard the screaming.

They'd be here soon.

They'd be here soon.

I ran toward the attic door. Gracie was pounding on the other side. I could hear her fingernails scraping along the door. "Hold on. Okay? My little brother's gone to get help. Calm down, okay? Don't hurt yourself."

"Can't help." The voice that didn't sound like Gracie's almost growled through the door.

The pounding stopped.

The scraping stopped.

The only thing I could hear was my breathing, hard, and fast. What was taking Mama and Mrs. Redding so long?

"Gracie, hold on? Hold—"

Screeching, like metal rubbing against metal, shot through the air. I couldn't place where it came from until I looked down and saw the doorknob moving ever so slowly.

I backed away. I was sure Gracie would come barreling out the door whenever she got free.

And I was right.

The door opened, and out dropped Gracie to her knees. Her hair sprang around her head like a bird's nest. Black mascara ran in rivers down her cheeks, and her black shirt had been ripped. Blood ran down her fingers from her broken nails.

Before I could move, Gracie grabbed me by the wrist and pulled me down to her. "I saw her. I saw her!"

"You saw who?" I examined her fingers. She needed a doctor, quick.

"Her," she repeated, which was no help. The attic door slammed shut, making both of us jump. Gracie scrambled down the hall and didn't stop until she ran into her mother at the top of the stairs.

CHAPTER FOURTEEN

I had never been more scared in my life.

It wasn't the house that scared me … okay maybe a little. And I wasn't afraid of the attic … okay, I was. What scared me so much was Gracie and how terrified she was, and how much her hands were bleeding.

Her mother got her downstairs, but once Gracie's feet hit the floor, she wouldn't budge. She rocked back and forth, talking about "her" … all about "her."

Mama grabbed me by the arm and glared. "What did you do to her?"

"Nothing. I promise." I didn't tell her that, originally, I had shut the door on her. It had been a simple prank, one I instantly regretted. But I hadn't done the other things. "I tried to help her."

The look on Mama's face made me realize that she didn't believe me. "Run upstairs and get her a blanket. Hurry."

I ran upstairs, and when I rounded the corner, every door, except my brother's, was open. I didn't take the time to think about it. I ran to my room, grabbed a blanket from the dresser, and raced down the stairs. Gracie's mother took the blanket from me. Her fingers were trembling, which made my heart sink. Mrs. Redding was as pale as Gracie. I felt horrible for all of it, but to be fair to myself, I hadn't invited Gracie over … and it was her idea to go ghost hunting.

"What can we do?" Mama asked, her fingers wrapped around her pink cell phone like she was ready to call 9-1-1.

"I think you've done enough," Gracie's mom said. Ouch. She helped Gracie up, made sure the blanket was secured around her shoulders, and led her to the front door.

"At least let us tend to her wounds," Mama offered.

"You've done enough!" her mother repeated loudly, making me jump.

Just as she made it to the door, it opened, making us all flinch at least a little bit.

My dad walked in with a few pizza boxes and two boxes of take-out in his hands. Once he saw the scene in front of him, he looked at my mom. "I can't leave this house for an hour before it all goes wrong?"

My mom rolled her eyes and stomped into the kitchen. Never had I heard my dad talk to my mom like that. Never had my mom stomped. What was wrong with them? What was wrong with this house?

"Ask your delinquent daughter," Mrs. Redding answered curtly as she pushed by my dad and led Gracie out the front door.

I did hope she would be all right, but again, I didn't invite her over. She knew the reputation of the house.

I still didn't know who "her" was, or what she'd seen in the attic that terrified Gracie so much.

"Okay," my dad drawled out once it was just him and me in the foyer. "Care to tell me what happened with your friend?"

"She's not my friend." Truer words had never been spoken.

"Is that why you invited her over? To scare her to death?" My mom came out of the kitchen, her arms folded across her chest.

Wait … "Are you accusing me of doing this to her on purpose?" I looked from her to my dad, whose brows were drawn together.

"Did what?" Dad huffed.

Mama answered for me. "Ava's friend, Gracie—"

"She's not my friend."

"Came over with her mother. She said that Ava had told her she could spend the night."

"I said I'd ask, but I wasn't planning on asking, because I didn't want her here."

"That's rude," Mama said like I'd kicked a dog or something.

"So is Gracie," I said.

Mama rolled her eyes. "She took her upstairs, 'cause Gracie wanted to see the architecture of the house—"

"She wanted to see ghosts," I corrected again.

"So, you decided to scare the poor girl to death?"

Mama's accusations hurt so bad. No, I hadn't meant to scare her on purpose. Okay, maybe I had at the beginning, but I didn't mean for her to get hurt.

"I didn't scare her!" How many more times did I have to say it?

"Then who did, Ava? Huh? Gracie kept repeating 'her' … 'her' … 'her' … who else in this place could it have possibly been? You are the only "her" here besides me, and I was downstairs with Mrs. Redding, who I hope doesn't decide to sue us for your behavior."

"Sue?" my dad chimed in behind us. "She can't do that for a child's prank."

"I didn't do anything," I added. No one listened to me.

"She has the connections, and people have gone to court over much less. Glory, Ava, what were you thinking?"

"I wasn't thinking—"

But Mama had already disappeared into the kitchen.

My dad followed obediently behind her, still holding supper.

Tears stung my eyes. Why couldn't they believe me? Why would Mama automatically assume that I'd done something to Gracie? I mean, okay, yeah, I had … kinda, but I didn't lock her in the attic. I wouldn't have.

Anxiety swirled in my stomach, and I ran out the door, through the grass, and didn't stop until I made it to Bradley's door.

CHAPTER FIFTEEN

Bradley's house wasn't far from mine, but normally I rode my bike. It defied understanding, but I got there quicker running—at least it felt that way to me.

The almost-full moon, called a Super Moon by the newscasters, hung over the sky like an ominous figure. A man watching our every move. Tomorrow, it would be at its peak, a once in a lifetime event, or so the newscasters said, too. The newscasters said a lot of things.

None of it pertained to me.

Though May, summer hadn't happened upon our little hamlet yet, not completely. The night was cool. The sweat that rolled down my face chilled my skin. My grandma would say I'd get sick sweating in the cool night air. She wasn't there to tell on me.

Once I caught my breath, I smelled cinnamon.

Images of a bakery full of treats swirled in my mind, but I knew that wasn't where the smell came from. Bradley's mom loved scented candles, and cinnamon was her favorite. Even though I didn't see her car in the driveway, I knew she was home. Neither Bradley—nor the babysitter—ever burned them when she wasn't around. Or so many. It had to be strong inside for me to smell it outside.

The streetlight hummed on the street. It flickered every so often, making the hairs on my arms stand up. Between my house and the streetlight, the hairs on my arms were getting quite the workout.

It had to be after nine. Dogs barked around the neighborhood, and most of the lights were out in the downstairs of the two-story houses. A few televisions flickered through the windows. Most of the adults were in bed. Since it was summer break, most of the kids were pretending to be.

I doubled over and put my hands on my knees, trying to think. The run happened in the blink of an eye, but the aftermath hit me hard.

Mama actually accused me of hurting Gracie on purpose. The nerve! I'd never …

What was I doing there?

Bradley's mama had to work the next day, and she didn't need me there that late.

I turned to leave just as the front door opened. Sure enough, it was Bradley. It was like he knew when I was around, like we had this connection or something—that he knew where I was, or if I were in trouble.

I was in trouble.

And I was there.

"Ava, is that you? I came out to get a bag my mom left in the car." He squinted through the light.

There went my busted bubble. "Yeah, sorry. I just came over."

"In the middle of the night?"

"It's barely nine." I might have been confused about a lot of things, but I wasn't confused about the time.

"Still … where's your bike?"

"I ran here."

"You ran … why?" He came down the first two steps, staring at me like I had five faces. He had on blue plaid pajamas that I'd never seen him wear, not that I'd seen him wear pajamas unless it was pajama day at school. Then he wore ninja turtle ones until last year when he opted for red plaid. At least he stayed in the plaid family. His black shirt was two sizes too big and fell in a lump around his shoulders. His hair curled in every way but the way it was supposed to.

And … he was barefoot.

I was still in my school clothes because I hadn't had time to change. I hadn't even been in my room since I'd been home. I hadn't had time. Most of my time had been in the attic or in the hallway with Gracie.

Gracie.

Tears stung my eyes when I thought about her, and my chest hurt from breathing so hard.

"Hey, Ava. What is it? What happened?" In three steps, he was down in front of me. Despite never really touching before, he pulled me into a hug. I had to have looked worse than I thought.

"I'm fine." I backed away before I wanted. Why did I come here? Had I really wanted Bradley to make me feel better? He thought the house was haunted in the first place. He'd probably laugh me out of the neighborhood.

"You're not fine."

"I am."

"Ava, don't. Don't break our pact."

Ouch. We'd had a pact since our first summer together. No matter what, we'd never lie to each other. A few larger-than-life tales, okay, but never lie.

I'd kept that promise, mostly.

"I'm not. I'm just … I want to be fine, all right? I don't even know why I came over. I just … you're busy, and I'm going to go." I turned to leave. Embarrassment caused me to hug myself and lower my head as I walked away as quickly as I could.

"It's the house, isn't it?" Bradley yelled, making me stop in my tracks. I couldn't turn around, couldn't look at him, but I couldn't lie to him, either.

"Gracie came over. She left bloody and bruised …"

"Gracie? What happened?" Bradley walked up behind me. I still didn't turn around. I didn't want him to see me like this.

"And my mom and dad are fighting. They never fight. Evan is acting all weird. Won't leave his room. Keeps talking to someone. And today, I lost it with Gracie, and she got hurt and—"

When Bradley stepped in front of me, my nose hit his chest. I took a step back, and thankfully, he didn't follow me. "Tell me exactly what happened. What was Gracie doing there? How did she get hurt?"

"I didn't do it." The words flew out of my mouth before I could stop them. "I … I mean, I wanted her to be quiet because she called me Dorkland like she used to. It slid out, you know, and I don't know, I got mad. Really mad, and I wanted her to pay, so I told her to go in the attic to look for ghosts, and I closed the door on her. Locked her in."

Bradley rocked back on his heels. "That doesn't seem that bad. Truthfully, she deserved it."

No, she didn't. "Then I couldn't get the door open. I tried and tried, but it wouldn't budge. It was like something was next to me, holding it shut. Gracie freaked out, started yelling about something in there with her, and when the door finally opened, her fingers were bleeding where she tried to claw her way out, and all she could say was, 'I saw her … I saw her.'" I shivered as the memory came rushing back. It was too raw, too fresh, and it hurt to think about.

"You didn't hurt her," Bradley said as calmly as he could. I could see the wheels turning in his head, though. He was trying to figure out the mystery, if there even was a mystery.

"I didn't save her," I countered. Had I expected Bradley to yell at me? I could have gotten that at home. I didn't know why I was there, but I was glad I was. I was glad Bradley knew, not that it would do any good.

"Bradley?" His mom, Susan, came out of the front door and wrapped her shawl around her shoulders. She had on only a light-pink nightgown and slippers. Her hair ran down her shoulders, laying in haphazard curls. "Ava? What in the world are you doing here at this time of night?"

Good question. How could I explain it to her without sounding crazy? I didn't even believe in ghosts, and I sounded crazy to me. "I got into a fight with my parents." A complete truth. "I had to get out and get some air. Ended up here."

"Twelve-year-olds shouldn't wander the streets at night 'getting air,'" Bradley's mom scolded. "Get in the car. I'm driving you home. You, too, Bradley. And don't you ever get it in your head to visit Ava's house at this hour, either."

"Don't worry," he said under his breath.

Bradley was deathly afraid of Mosley Manor. Turned out, he'd been the smart one.

CHAPTER SIXTEEN

I f the run to Bradley's house had been the shortest of all time, the drive back was the longest. His mom hadn't changed clothes. She'd just grabbed her bag, and we piled in her car. Bradley and I sat in the back seat, both on opposite sides. Every so often, I noticed him looking at me. I didn't know what he was thinking. I didn't want to know. It was probably something about he told me so, how the house was hurting people, how it was all my fault, though Bradley was nice and would never say something like that out loud.

The silence cut through the car like a knife. His mama didn't even have on the radio to make the awkward silence less awkward.

As we got closer to my house, my stomach churned. Like before, every light in the house was on … even the one in the attic—the one I hadn't known was there.

Bradley's mom slowed in front of the house and put the car into park. A long sigh echoed through the car from the front seat as Bradley and I glanced at each other in the back. "Ava, your parents are going to be worried sick."

If we still lived in our old house, I'd believe her. As it was, I wasn't sure.

"Do you want me to go in with you? Make sure everything is okay? Maybe tell them where you were, you know, if you need some sort of backup?"

All in all, I liked Bradley's mama. She treated me like the daughter she never had—most of the time. I didn't blame her, though. Any parent would have freaked at the sight of a twelve-year-old in their yard in the night.

Curious, I looked over at Bradley, who had his eyes trained on the house. He'd grown a little paler since we'd stopped. I didn't blame him.

I didn't want to scare him more, either. "I'll be okay." I went for the door.

Bradley reached for my arm to stop me. "We can come in with you. If you want. You didn't just run to my house for the exercise."

"Says who?" I tried to laugh it off. More than anything, I was just tired and wanted to sleep … if I could sleep.

"It's not funny," Bradley said. He was right. It wasn't funny. None of it was. It was my life, and I couldn't believe it.

"You know …" I started speaking without really knowing why. "I've never been afraid of this house. Ever. I've always loved the history of it. The stories of Old Man Mosley and the families who lived here before. I knew there was no evidence of ghosts because there aren't … ghosts. Period. Then I moved in … and bam … All these things started happening, and I don't understand it. There has to be a logical explanation."

"What if the logical explanation is ghosts?" Bradley so helpfully asked.

"What do you think, Ms. Susan? Do you believe in ghosts?"

She shrugged. "I don't know, but what I do know is you.

You wouldn't let this house do this to you if there wasn't something to it."

Something to it. That didn't make me feel any better.

"I'll talk to you tomorrow." I opened the door, and my stomach lurched as the wind hit my leg. I really didn't want to go back inside, but I had to. My family was in there, and I couldn't stay out here forever. "Thank you for driving me home. I'm sorry to have bothered you."

"No bother. I can go in if you want."

"No," I answered a bit too forcefully. Truthfully, I didn't want anything to happen to Susan or Bradley. I didn't trust the house.

I didn't trust me.

CHAPTER SEVENTEEN

I went through the house, looking for Mama and Daddy and flipping the lights off in the empty rooms as I passed by. I knew we didn't have much money, and wasting money on electricity wouldn't help anything.

Nobody was in the living room. The only things of any interest in there were a can of yellow paint and half a pizza left in the box.

The kitchen wasn't any better. Take-out boxes were thrown all over the floor. Cans of soda littered the counter. One had been turned over, and the caramel-colored drink slowly slid down the counter. Quickly, I went to tip it back up, rummaged around until I found a paper towel, and cleaned up the spill. What in the world was going on?

My parents would never have left a mess like that. Ever. They weren't the tidiest people in the world. No one would ever eat off our floors, but that was kind of the point, no one would eat off our floors. So why were the food boxes there, thrown around like they had been flung at someone? Why hadn't the drinks been thrown away? What had happened while I'd been gone?

"Mama?" I yelled, not caring if she'd ground me when she found me. I would have even settled for a lecture on running away. I just wanted to see her, make sure she was okay.

No answer.

Where were they? They couldn't have just disappeared. From the looks of the kitchen, it seemed like a food fight broke out, but that was stupid because my parents wouldn't have done that.

"Mama!" I ran through the kitchen, jumping over wasted boxes and spilled food, and around the foyer through the study. I stopped at my parents' bedroom door. The room hadn't originally been a bedroom, I didn't think, but it was the room they had chosen as theirs so Evan and I could have different rooms. We had appreciated that at the time.

I hesitated before I knocked on the door. What if they were still mad? They had every right to be. What if they didn't want to see me? What if they were asleep, and I woke them up and ticked them off more? Then again, why would they be sleeping if I had run away? Wouldn't they have come after me or something? Stayed up and made sure I'd made it home?

Unless I'd really messed up, and my parents hated me.

A cold tingle ran from the tips of my toes, all the way up my body, and through my head. What if they hated me … what if they didn't want me to come back? What if … what if they were happy I was gone and went to sleep peacefully, glad to have me away from them?

My fist trembled as I held it, unsure whether to knock or not. Turned out, I didn't have to decide. The door opened ever so slowly. I thought Mama was doing it, but when the door kept opening and whining on its hinges, I saw Mama and Daddy. She was asleep in the chair, covered in her grandma's old blanket. It had been their covers on their bed in the rental house.

My dad lay with his back to my mom in the bed. He had an old, tattered blanket over him and curled into a ball. Apparently, they were as irritated at each other as they were me. It broke my heart.

At least they were asleep, though. That meant I could crash. I was sleepy enough to sleep. I hoped my eyes and brain cooperated.

I left their door open and quietly tiptoed through the study and up the stairs, not wanting to wake them.

Evan's door was slightly open, and I peeked in to see if I saw anything. All I could see was an old wooden bookshelf. Nothing exciting. No sign of Evan, though I did hear breathing in there, so I assumed he was all right.

"Goodnight, Evan."

I listened carefully, barely breathing, so I could hear if he answered back. I stayed longer than I had in Mama and Daddy's room. I didn't think Evan had any reason to be mad at me, so when he didn't answer, I made myself assume that it was because he was asleep.

Exhausted, I made my way to the bathroom and quickly brushed my teeth and got ready for bed. The attic door was open when I crossed the hallway to my room. I didn't close it. I didn't care. I was too tired.

I threw my covers on the old mattress and climbed under the soft, warm fabric. I wanted to sleep, but in the darkness of the room, my mind wouldn't shut off. Was I in a haunted house? Did I believe in haunted houses? What was going on with my parents? Was buying a new house really that stressful?

Would we ever get back to normal?

I wished it wasn't summer. I wished I could go to school and get away from the house for a little while. I wished so many things.

As I wished, my eyes grew heavier and heavier. Soon, I could barely open my eyes, and I felt myself being drawn into nothingness.

CHAPTER EIGHTEEN

There's a noise outside, talking. Outside my door. I lay very still, looking up at the ceiling and listening. The ceiling looks different somehow, new, not with water stains or even mold. There's fresh paint up there, and I wonder if Mama and Daddy had time to paint today.

The sound of splashing water makes me jump straight up in my bed. The hairs on the back of my head stand on end as I listen. That's coming from the bathroom.

There's yelling.

"Lay down! David! I have to do this before Father comes home. Lay still!" It's a girl. I don't recognize her voice, but she sounds somewhere around my age.

As quietly as I can, I roll out of bed, careful not to have my feet make the floorboards squeak, and slowly head for the door.

The hallway is the same, mostly. Like my room, it looks new. The wallpaper isn't torn. The rug doesn't have those dark-brown stains on it, and there is a table with a very alive plant sitting across the hall from Evan's room.

I'm dreaming. I have to be. Either that or I slept way longer than I thought, and my parents have been very busy.

"David, stop splashing!"

I tiptoe to the bathroom and peek through the barely opened door. A girl in a white dress with a white apron over it is kneeling next to the bathtub. She's trying her hardest to wash the flopping boy, who looks a little younger than Evan. He still has all his clothes on as he splashes, a fact she doesn't seem happy about. "David, Father is going to kill me. He told me not to let you get dirty, and what do you do? Sneak out of the house and go playing in the mud! And then track it all over the house like some sort of animal. Do you know what he'll do to me if I don't get this clean? Do you?" Her voice is harsh, terrified. The quicker she speaks, the faster she scrubs David. Finally, he gives in and stops fighting.

"I'll help you clean, Rachel. I'm sorry."

"You're sorry … you're sorry. I'm the one who's going to be sorry." Rachel is nearly frantic as she scrubs harder. David cries out, and she eases up … "I'm sorry." She throws the rag down in the tub and backs away. "I'm sorry I hurt you. I'm just …"

"You're afraid of him," David answers for her. He stands in the water and starts to unbutton his shirt. "We'll hide these clothes in the attic. I'll help you wash them tomorrow. I'll wash up, and you clean the kitchen. He'll never notice. He hasn't been getting home until after dark all month."

Just as he says it, just as the words are out of his mouth, the front door opens. Rachel looks at David; fear fills her eyes.

"What in the world?" A large bass voice booms from the first floor. "Rachel Mosley! What have you done!"

"Father." As Rachel stands, her legs shake. "He's going to brand me for sure."

"I'll talk to him. I'll take the blame. It was my fault, after all." David places one foot on the floor. It's wet and soapy, slippery. "I won't let him hurt you."

"Rachel!" Their father's voice barrels through the hallway. Even I flinch. What will he do when he sees me? I can't run and hide. All I can do is stand and watch like I'm watching a memory. His footsteps *pound with each step as he goes closer and closer to the second floor. Rachel is frozen, her eyes wide, and her fingers are gripping the sink so hard her knuckles are turning white.*

"I won't let him hurt you," David promises as he steps out of the tub. The floor is slippery from all the water and soap. His feet fly out from under him. Rachel and I both jump as the back of his head cracks against the bathtub.

I sat up so quickly, my head spun. My heart felt like it was going to burst out of my chest.

My eyes scanned the room quickly, and I listened very hard for footsteps pounding up the stairs. Her father was coming … he was going to hurt her … he was …

A nightmare.

It had only been a nightmare.

Everything in my room looked just like it had when I went to sleep. The mold ring was back on my ceiling. Funny how that comforted me. The sun streamed through the window. It was daylight. No more dream. No more Rachel and David Mosley.

"Mosley," I mumbled to myself. It had to be nothing, my mind playing tricks on me. The only person I knew who lived in the house was Old Man Mosley, and he'd been gone for years. Of course, someone could have lived there before him and probably had, but why had I dreamed about them?

"It was only a dream," I told myself, but it felt like a lie. That was the most real dream I'd ever had in my life. Every detail, every smell, every emotion felt real. Like I was watching a memory instead of having a nightmare. To make myself feel better, I decided to ask Bradley if he wanted to go to the library and research the house. Maybe find out if someone had died there. It made me cringe to even think about it.

Me. Ava Kirkland. Considering the possibility that there were actual ghosts in the house.

What happened to me?

The smell of pancakes broke me from my ghost ponderings. Not long after, I smelled bacon. Someone was cooking breakfast. Oh, yeah, I was up for that.

I grabbed my kitten house shoes and raced out of my room. Evan's door was closed. Big shocker. Maybe he was already downstairs. He loved pancakes more than I did.

When I made it to the kitchen, Evan was nowhere to be found. Daddy was manning the stove. I was glad it actually worked. And Mama, well Mama, stood with her arms crossed, glaring at me from the doorway.

"Told you pancakes would make her come running," Daddy said.

I hated I was that predictable. "Look, I'm sorry about last night. Everything was weird, and I ran to Bradley's house. His mom brought me home, but you two were already asleep."

"We heard you come in," Mama said, unblinking.

Okay then … "Anyway, I am sorry, and I'll never do anything like that again."

"Oh, I know you won't," Mama answered, her head tilted to the side, and it had to be a play of the light because it looked like her eyes flashed blue. But that was impossible. "How could you?"

"How could I what?" Mama's eyes grew three sizes bigger as she marched toward me. I'd never in my life seen her that mad. "Look, I'm sorry I left. I really am, but I won't do it again. I swear."

"Don't swear. It's not what civilized people do, Rachel."

Rachel ...

She grabbed me by the arm and dragged me to the living room. She pointed to the floor. I saw nothing. She saw everything. "Mud, Rachel! Who is going to clean up all the mud?"

CHAPTER NINETEEN

"There's no mud. There's no mud, Mama." My voice shook as I spoke. My arm hurt where she gripped me so hard. What was wrong with her?

"There is mud!" she screamed as her fingernails bit into the sensitive skin under my arm, making me flinch. "You and your brother know better."

"My brother hasn't left his room in days," I countered. "And my name isn't Rachel."

Mama pulled me up so I could see her eye to eye. I hadn't been wrong before. Her normally brown irises were bright blue. "I warned you. Now you leave me no choice."

She started to pull me, and it didn't hit me where until we reached the foyer and started up the stairs. "No, please … please. I'll clean up the mud. I'll clean it up." I didn't see it, but I could pretend. Until I figured it out, I could pretend.

"It's too late, Rachel. I'm not telling you to clean up this mess again."

I grabbed the banister, and it groaned and popped under my weight. "Daddy! Help me!" My gaze caught his through the spokes in the banister railing. He stood in the kitchen—pancakes in hand. His eyes were white.

Completely white.

"No." The whisper caught in my throat. My fingers hesitated just enough to let go of the banister, and Mama dragged me up the steps. I clawed and grabbed at every step I could, but I couldn't get a grip on her.

No, this wasn't her. It wasn't her … It was too much like my nightmare. Mama's eyes had changed, and it wasn't from contacts. Not that quickly.

There was no way … no way.

My brother's stupid door was shut again, but I wasn't about to try to get him to help me. He didn't need in this mess.

"I warned you," Mama said again. She dragged me down the hallway.

The attic door was open, and my blood ran cold. I didn't want to go up there. I needed to run out of the house, go to Bradley's, and get some help. Mama needed help. We all needed help. Who would help? Who knew how to get rid of ghosts?

It had to be a ghost, some sort of possession because this wasn't my mother. I knew that. I knew …

We halted suddenly in front of the bathroom. The door was wide open, and when I saw the scene inside, I dropped to my knees.

My brother, my sweet brother, laid in the middle of the bathroom floor. His head was propped up against the tub like he had slipped and fallen. Blood oozed from around his ears. His eyes were shut.

"What did you do?" Mama asked, her tone cold.

"I didn't …" I couldn't get the words out. I couldn't take my eyes off of Evan. A nightmare. Maybe I hadn't woken up

from my nightmare, not really, and this was part of it. Right
… Right!?

Water mixed with blood streamed from the tub and down
toward the door, toward me.

This couldn't be happening.

"Evan."

"David!" Mama cried.

David … David and Rachel.

Mama thought we were the kids from my nightmare.

The boy who got hurt.

The girl … what happened to the girl?

Automatically, my eyes slid toward the attic door, and I
knew, I knew without being told. I knew what was about to
happen.

Mama pulled me up by my shirt. Her bright-blue, unnat-
ural, eyes were wide and frightening. "You did this."

"I didn't." I barely got the words out.

"You killed David!" She pushed me backward, still
holding onto my shirt.

Killed … he wasn't dead. Evan wasn't dead!

"He needs help. Mama, we need to get him help."

"Stop calling me that, Rachel. Your mother, God rest her
soul, can't help you now." She pushed me out of the bathroom and down the hall until the backs of my ankles touched
the stairs leading up to the attic.

"I know you are in there, Mama." My rational brain had
left, and all I was left with was the fact that someone, Rachel
and David's father, most likely, had taken over my mother.
That we were living out some sort of echo of what had
happened that night. I saw the claw marks on the attic door,
and my stomach lurched. No … no. "Mama, stop. This isn't
you."

Mama pushed me hard, and I landed on the stairs hard.

"You're right. It isn't your mama. She's not here anymore."

The door slammed.

The key locked.

I was surrounded by darkness.

CHAPTER TWENTY

"Mama!" I banged on the door so loud it echoed in my ears. "Mama, open the door! I'm sorry! I'll clean it up. The mud. Just let me out! Call an ambulance for Evan!"

Bang.

Bang.

Bang.

"Please!" I kicked the door as hard as I could and twisted the knob. It wouldn't budge.

What am I going to do? What am I going to do?

First thing I had to do was get up off the steps and to the actual attic floor. There was a window up there, and if I could see, it might help a little bit. At least let me stop and breathe.

Carefully, I crawled on all fours up the stairs and didn't stop until I'd made it past the mirror, past the totes, and to the window. It was one of the only ones my parents hadn't taken the boards off of, but thankfully, for me, there were a few slits in the wood that allowed light to come in and me to see out.

It was something. I took it.

Leaning on the window like it was my lifeline, I closed my eyes and focused on my breathing. Freaking out wouldn't do anybody any good.

I needed help. That was the most important thing. Well, the most important thing was that Evan needed help. I didn't care what that 'thing' said that had taken over Mama. He wasn't dead. He couldn't be. To get Evan help, I needed to get out of the attic, and to do that I needed …

I drew a blank.

What did I need?

I needed a miracle; that's what I needed.

I banged my head against the wood in frustration and heard glass breaking. I raised up and noticed that my little head injury broke some of the glass out. I could yell for help if I wanted, not that anyone was around to hear me.

"Not much fun, is it?"

I turned around and saw the sheet had moved from the mirror, and it wasn't my reflection staring back at me.

A girl around my age, wearing a white dress with a white apron stood looking at me through the mirror glass. Her hair was messy all around her head, and she was incredibly pale. I knew her, I'd seen her in my nightmare.

My nightmare that I felt like I was still in.

"Rachel?" I asked, trying my best not to freak out.

She nodded.

Well, then.

"How do I get out of here?"

She laughed, actually laughed. "You don't. You stay here. You get cold. You get hungry. You get thirsty." She paused as if lost in some distant memory. "You get sleepy. Then you don't get anything."

"You died up here."

Again, she nodded.

That most certainly didn't make me feel good. "Your dad locked you in?"

"Yes."

"For making a mess with the mud?"

She tilted her head quizzically. "For killing my brother."

A whimper escaped my lips as my head raced. From what I saw in the nightmare/memory, her brother had slipped. She hadn't had anything to do with it. "He fell," I tried to reassure her.

"He hit his head."

"He slipped."

"On the soap I spilled."

"He tracked in the mud."

"I should have been watching him more closely."

"You're just a little girl." I felt the rage pumping through my veins. How dare her father put so much pressure on her! "It wasn't your fault."

Rachel flinched in the mirror, and for a few seconds, didn't look at me. When she finally did again, her eyes were watery. I didn't even know ghosts could cry. I mean, up until about an hour ago, I didn't believe they existed. "Yes, it is."

It broke my heart to hear her say it. No, it wasn't her fault. None of it was. She'd simply been trying to take care of her brother when an accident happened. That was all. She shouldn't have had to die for it.

"Your father … he never came back for you?"

She shook her head. "He'd locked me in here before when I'd done bad things. Maybe overnight, maybe for two. Never more than two." She said that like it was a good thing. It made my stomach hurt. People didn't do that to their kids. Ever. "But he never came back. And I couldn't get out. I went to sleep then … I woke up in this mirror."

"Ghosts go into mirrors?" I'd never heard of that before

… wait, I had. I'd heard about how people used to put sheets or cloth over mirrors if a dead body was close by so the glass wouldn't soak up the spirit of the person. There was no way there was any truth to that, though. Or maybe. I mean, I was standing there, talking to a ghost in a mirror.

"Spirits" —she corrected— "can attach to things. I saw this light, and I knew what it meant. Somehow, despite my sinful ways, despite killing my brother, I was being summoned to Heaven." Rachel swallowed hard. "But I couldn't go. I couldn't leave my brother. I didn't know if he was still here or what happened to him, but I couldn't leave him. So, I latched onto this mirror. Then I got stuck. And my brother, he got stuck on the second floor."

"Then who is possessing my parents?" A sentence I never thought I'd ask anyone, much less a ghost in a mirror.

Rachel sucked in a breath that I was sure she didn't need. "I'm afraid to tell you."

"Rachel, whoever it is, I need to know. I've got to protect my family."

She shook her head. "I'm not sure. I've already disappointed him once."

"And look what that did for you." I regretted sounding so cruel. I calmed myself and tried to be understanding. "Rachel, please. Please. Help me save my family. Please tell me who is possessing my parents."

Rachel hesitated again. I could see her fighting with herself, trying to figure out what the right thing to do was. Finally, she opened her mouth and closed her eyes. Her words came out fast and furious. "Father, I think. He's the reason I've never left the attic. I can't. He won't let me."

Her father. I was glad she told me, but the hair on my neck stood on end. I couldn't imagine a father being so cruel.

"And now he won't let me," I replied.

I wanted to beat down that door so hard and do—something—I didn't know what. I couldn't hurt her dad, not as long as he was in control of my mom. My own dad was a dead end. He had been taken over by something, too, and hadn't been any help while I'd been hauled up here. My brother—was going to be fine. I needed out, though.

I needed a miracle.

Pounding echoed from the walls downstairs, like someone had been knocking on the door for a very long time and had gotten frustrated. I peeked through the wooden slats covering the now broken window and didn't see anybody. A few seconds later, I noticed Bradley backing away from the door.

Bradley!

My miracle!

"Bradley!" I screamed as loud as I could as I beat on the window, anything for him to know I was there. "Bradley, up here!"

Bradley turned and walked toward the road, his hands in his pockets and his head down in defeat. What had Mama told him? What had she done to send him away like that?

"Bradley!" I yelled so loudly, my throat hurt. I beat the window until my hand turned blue.

All at once, Bradley stopped and turned toward the house.

"Up here, Bradley! Please!" I beat harder and harder on the window.

Bradley looked up, and if he saw me, he didn't show it. Instead, he lowered his head and grabbed his bike.

"No! Bradley, don't go! Don't. I'm up here! I'm up here! Don't leave me!"

I watched as Bradley got on his bike and disappeared down the street toward his house.

Leaving me all alone.

Rachel giggled from the mirror. "You're not alone. You have me. Forever and always."

I slid down to the floor and pulled my knees to my chest. I had to get out of here, but it seemed my one miracle had come and gone.

CHAPTER TWENTY-ONE

"How long have you been here?" I asked to make conversation. I wasn't sure how long I'd been in that attic, but it seemed like forever already. Sometime, the sun would go down, and I'd be stuck in here, in the dark. I shivered when I thought about it and tried very hard not to dwell on the idea. I'd get out of here before it got dark. I had to. Evan needed me.

My parents needed me.

Rachel seemed to think. "I'm not sure. I was born in nineteen-hundred-twenty-eight."

"Nineteen—wow, that was a long time ago."

"Is it?"

"Yeah, like almost a century, give or take a decade or two."

"A century!" It was her turn to act surprised. "I can't imagine everything that's gone on out there. It seems so strange to think about ever being out of this room."

"What about Old Man Mosley? Did you know him?"

She smiled affectionately. There was no other way to describe it. "You mean Jacob?"

I did mean Jacob.

"He was my brother."

Her brother? "Wait, I thought your brother was David. The boy who died in the bathroom."

The light left her eyes, and a dark shadow covered her. Sorta wished I hadn't brought him up. "David was my younger brother. Jacob was my older brother. He was away during the war until everything happened."

"Then he came home?"

"Yes, to take care of the funerals and the home. He never left, though. Never. I think he knew we were here."

"He never saw you?"

She shook her head, then narrowed her brows. "When he was getting the house ready to sell, I heard him on the second floor, talking to someone. I think he saw David, but I can't be sure. He couldn't bear coming up here. This is where they found my body, and, well, he felt responsible."

"Why? He was away at war. There was nothing he could have done."

"He knew how Father was. And he left us with him." Rachel sounded bitter, and I didn't really blame her. Not that her brother left. It wasn't his job to take care of them, but that her father was so cruel and hurt them so badly.

"I knew he was here, though, and that meant the world to me. I can't leave the mirror, but I can hear what's going on."

"And where was your father this whole time?"

"I'm not sure. Not entirely. I know he didn't come around until Jacob left. Then there was no one to keep him away, and he loved that."

"I'm so sorry Jacob died and got to move on, and you are stuck here." I felt like crying at the injustice of it all. This girl had done nothing wrong and had suffered so long because of a monster who called himself her father.

"Jacob didn't die," she said, surprising me.

"What? Yes, he did. A few years ago. That's why my parents bought the house."

She shook her head. "No, I heard them. He didn't want to leave, but someone said he had to. They said it wasn't safe for him to be here by himself. He said he couldn't leave his siblings …" She stopped, then looked up at me. "His siblings. I forgot he'd said that. He did know we were here. He was protecting us the only way he knew how, and then when he left—"

"Your dad came back."

"My dad came back." She meant her daddy's spirit, I know she did. Her jaw clenched, and I could feel the tension and anger in her voice. "I miss my brother. Even though I couldn't see him. Even though I couldn't talk to him, I knew he was here. It was comforting to know he was here, and I didn't want to leave him."

I slid up on my knees, my brain whirling with an idea. "Rachel, do you think if I broke the mirror, you could get out?"

"Maybe, but who knows what would happen to me? Would I get to stay here with David? Would I go to Heaven? Would I … not go to Heaven?" She shivered.

I got her meaning. "Honestly, I don't know. But—" I jumped up. It had to work. It had to, for all of us.

"What are you doing?"

"I have a plan to help us all out."

She stood straighter, her shoulders back. "What do you need?"

I let out a shaky breath. This was it. All or nothing. "A miracle," I answered.

CHAPTER TWENTY-TWO

These were the things I knew for sure:

One, the door was locked from the outside.

Two, I couldn't break the door down.

Three, I couldn't claw my way out.

Four, and most importantly, I had to get out of the attic.

The window was broken out, so I could see the road. I could yell at anyone for help, if they would listen. Not like Bradley heard me, though, so that was a negative. I didn't know if Evan was still lying in the bathroom, bleeding, but I had to consider he was, which meant the urgency to get out of the house was so much greater.

I had a plan for *after* I got out. The actual getting out of the room was the problem.

Think, I had to think.

The attic was empty except for the few boxes that had dust an inch thick on them. If Rachel hadn't been able to get out of the room using whatever was in them, then I didn't think I'd have much luck, either. I couldn't go out the door. I knew that. But what about …

I ran to the tub Mama had brought up here earlier and flipped the lid off.

"What are you doing?" Rachel asked from the mirror.

"Looking." I yanked out my backpack and unzipped it. Surely, there was something in there that could help me. The window was boarded up from the inside. Why, I didn't know, but it was, so I had to deal with it. The glass was broken, so I could conceivably climb out—if the wood was gone.

Now how to remove the wood?

I poured the contents of my backpack out in the little stream of light that came through the glass. Math book, something I most certainly didn't need. Ruler. Protractor. Calculator. Binders. Nothing useful. Nothing that could help me.

Frustrated, I pulled out Evan's bag without any sort of hope that I'd find anything. My big grand idea to get out was starting to fall apart, because I couldn't find anything to pull the wood from the window.

Wait …

I poured out all of Evan's stuff on the floor next to mine. Books, notebooks, basically the same as mine, except … he had an art project in his.

I forgot the third graders made them for their moms for Mother's Day, and, apparently, Evan had forgotten, too. It was a wind chime, just a simple wind chime with a hanger for the top and little pieces of painted metal hanging down from it. Each cylinder of metal was sturdy and round and just might work.

Not wanting to overthink it, I carried the wind chime to the window and wedged one of my binders under the wood next to a nail. A huge part of my scientific brain said this would not work, but a bigger part knew that it had to work. However, if for some reason it didn't, I'd find something else.

I wouldn't give up. I wouldn't end up dead and in the mirror with Rachel.

With the binder in place, I used the metal as a lever to push the binder up. The idea was to loosen or break the nail and move it away from the window. Apparently, I used a lot of upper-body strength, because the only thing that popped was the binder. What had I expected? It was made of plastic, and metal was a lot stronger than plastic.

I threw my binder down and ran my fingers through my hair. This was stupid. "Why didn't you try to go out the window when you were in here?" I asked Rachel. "I mean, you could have. Seemed smarter than clawing at the door." I remembered those claw marks, seeing the blood on my fingers, on Gracie's fingers ... when I looked closer at Rachel, I saw them on her fingers in the mirror.

"I thought about it. I did. I was afraid Father would get even madder at me for breaking the window, though, so I didn't. Once I decided he wasn't coming back, I don't know ... I should have. I should have tried."

"Hindsight," I told her. It was what my mom used to say when something didn't go as planned, or I learned something the hard way. Hindsight—the act of seeing what you should have done only when the event was in the past. As in, I never should have moved into this house ... Hindsight.

Okay, I couldn't use the binder. That had been not so smart. If it had worked, it would have been genius. I had the metal, which was a great lever, though, so what else could I use?

"Break the mirror," Rachel said, surprising me.

"What?"

"Break the mirror. Use the metal around it to open the window. It would work, wouldn't it?"

"I think so, but you said you didn't know what would happen to you if the mirror broke."

"I know what will happen to you if you don't."

I looked at her, running all of this through my head. It was too much, all of it was too much. It was summer, and I was twelve. I should have been riding bikes with Bradley, swimming, reading, doing anything besides being up in this attic, talking to a ghost in a mirror about possibly sending her into oblivion. "I don't want you to get hurt."

She laughed bitterly. "I'm a ghost. How more hurt can I be?"

She had a point. Didn't mean I liked it. "I don't know."

"Can you break the glass or not?"

I glanced down at the metal rod in my hand. "I can."

"And after you break it, can you get the metal off and use it to open the window?"

"I think so, but—"

"No buts. Just do it." She backed away.

Slowly, I walked toward her. The metal in my hand grew slick with sweat. I didn't want to do this.

My fingers trembled, and the rod was difficult to hold. "I don't want to hurt you," I said.

"You won't." She smiled, her lips trembling.

I wrapped my fingers around the metal rod and held it up like a bat. It wasn't very big, maybe the length of my forearm, but it would do enough damage to do what needed to be done.

"Are you ready?"

"Yes," she answered as she covered her eyes with her hand.

"Are you scared?"

She hesitated only briefly. "Yes," she replied as my metal rod slammed into the mirror, busting it into a hundred pieces.

Rachel was gone.

I had to work fast.

CHAPTER TWENTY-THREE

"Rachel?" I asked into the nothingness, just to be certain she wasn't around. With her limited ghost body, she couldn't have done anything except be moral support. Moral support sounded nice.

I didn't see her anywhere. Great. I was on my own.

"You can do this." I bent some metal off the mirror, which wasn't an easy task. I pushed and pulled, all the while trying not to cut my fingers on the glass laying around everywhere. Too bad I couldn't have used it to get out of the window.

Once I had a fairly sharp piece of metal from the frame, I went to the window and wedged it under the wood. I said a little prayer and used the other metal piece from the wind chime to push down on the metal from the mirror. When I didn't think I could push anymore, the nail groaned.

I nearly did a dance of joy. "Did you see that, Rachel?" I guess I hoped Rachel was still there, somewhere. I didn't want to think of her as gone, especially since it was me who broke her mirror. I couldn't dwell on that now. I had to get out. Pushing the metal harder, I nearly fell through the glass when both nails on that side budged at the same time. Splinters of wood flew around me, and I shielded my eyes. When I opened them, the board swung on two nails. I had enough room to get out.

"Woohoo!" I said, then covered my mouth. I didn't know where my parents were, and I didn't want them to know what I was doing. I had a plan, after all.

I grabbed Evan's backpack and put my hand inside for protection. Holding my breath, I smashed my hand through the glass that hadn't broken yet, shattering pieces everywhere. Thank goodness, none of it cut me. I'd been lucky. Yup, totally my lucky day.

I had an opening. I just had to take it. I hoped the roof to the porch held me because if it didn't, it would be a long, hard fall down to the ground.

"This is a bad idea," I told myself as I slid my leg out through the window, careful not to slide it across any glass. What else could I do? I had to get help. I had to get out. "Bye, Rachel. Thank you." I hoped she could hear me wherever she was.

The roof to the porch was another story down. I had to make a choice, grab the gutters that looked like they'd seen better days, and climb down, or jump to the roof and roll, somehow to the ground. If I did that, I'd probably break my neck. I'd most definitely break my leg. I hadn't planned this out well. I'd made it through the window. Yay me. Now I needed a way to get down.

What did I need to do?

"Rachel!" Mama's voice boomed from the hallway. I jumped and nearly lost my balance. I grabbed onto the windowsill and sliced my palms with glass. I couldn't hold in the yelp.

"Rachel!" Mama called again. "You better not be doing anything up there. I heard noises."

"Crap." With time running out and no other choices, I

slid out the window and landed hard on the roof. If Mama didn't know where I was before, she sure did after hearing my body land on the tin roof. I left a dent like I was a rock hitting the roof of a car. Everything hurt. I hadn't broken my leg, but my spleen was an entirely different story.

"Rachel!" Mama's voice boomed so loud the house shook, literally. Things were going down fast, and I had to get help. With no time to lose, I turned and rolled to the left, where I hoped there was one thing that would save my fall. I closed my eyes, held my breath, and suddenly, I was flying through the air. In a freefall, but still, flying.

It was almost peaceful for a moment, until I hit the branches of a bush I'd hoped would break my fall. I hit every branch on the way down, each stick clawing and slicing at my skin. By the time I rolled out and put my feet on solid ground, I looked and felt like I'd been attacked by twenty angry cats. I looked myself over and didn't see any major damage, except for scrapes and blood. My left hand had a piece of glass hanging out of it that I yanked out. Blinding pain erupted from my toes to the top of my head. Stupid, stupid idea. I thought I'd be sick.

No time to be sick. I tossed the red-smeared piece of glass down on the grass and tried not to think about the pain. Rachel needed me. My family needed me. I had to get help.

I took a step, and a hand landed on my shoulder. I started to yell, and another hand grabbed my mouth. I fought to kick whoever it was off. I hadn't gone this long and this hard to get caught now.

"Shhhh …" a voice whispered in my ear.

I didn't want to "shhhh." I kicked backwards as hard as I could, my heel connecting with something solid. My attacker let me go with a groan, and when I turned around, I saw Bradley doubled over.

"Oh my gosh! I'm so sorry." I tried to go over and help him, but he held his hand up to keep me away.

"I'm all right."

"I thought we promised never to lie to each other."

He sighed. "It hurts really bad."

"Sorry." And I was. I'd also never been so happy to see anyone in my life. "Come on. We need to go. I have to find him."

"Who?" He sprinted behind me.

"Jacob Mosley. He's the only one who can help."

CHAPTER TWENTY-FOUR

B radley helped me to his house. He threw one of my arms around his shoulder, and he held onto me around the waist. If any of the neighbors saw us running back toward his house from mine, they didn't come out and say anything.

We were out of breath by the time we reached his front porch. He helped me sit down and catch my breath and went inside to get his mother.

He figured his mother could solve anything. I used to think mine could, too.

No, that wasn't fair. My mother hadn't abandoned me. She'd been taken over, and possession and active abandonment were two different things. Deep down, somewhere inside her, my mother was there, and she had to be fighting to get out.

I leaned my head against the banister and shut my eyes. I tried to relax and breathe, but every time I closed my eyes, all I saw was Rachel in the mirror, and Evan on the bathroom floor with blood oozing out from around him.

Evan!

I should have stopped at one of the neighbors' houses to

use their phone and call an ambulance for Evan. I hadn't exactly forgotten, but I'd wanted out of that house so bad I didn't think about it. I wanted the safety of Bradley's house. I wanted the comfort of his mother.

I shouldn't have forgotten him, though.

The front door creaked on its hinges as Bradley's mama came barreling out. "Ava, are you all right?" She raced down the steps and sat down beside me. Before I could say anything, she took my face in her hands and examined me. "Look up," she said, so I did as she pulled my bottom eyelid down. "Now, look down." So, I did that, too. I was grateful Bradley's mama was a nurse.

I shook her hands off me and stood up as quickly as I could. A nurse! She could help us.

All good intentions aside, once I stood, I got all dizzy and woozy. I had to grab onto Bradley's mama to keep from falling over.

"You need to sit down," she ordered in her most adult voice.

I wasn't in any place to argue, so I plopped back down. The bruises on my bottom and my back hurt so bad. Falling off a roof and into a bush tended to do that.

"What happened to her?" I assumed she was talking to Bradley. "Grab some bandages for her hands."

"Fell off her roof," he answered as he ran inside and quickly ran back out with some of his mom's flamingo dish towels I'd gotten her for Christmas a few years ago. He tossed them to his mom, who held them on my wounds.

"We need to get her to the emergency room. She could have internal bleeding. Does this hurt?" She put her hand on my side, right at my ribcage, and told me to breathe in. So, I did. And I instantly regretted it.

"Like I said. Possible internal bleeding. Bradley, call an ambulance."

"No," I grunted and tried to stand again.

"Ava …"

"No, listen. I'm not the only one hurt. Evan is in the bathroom. He's bleeding really bad. He needs help."

"Where are your parents?"

I didn't want to tell her. She would never believe me anyway. "Gone." Which wasn't a lie. It wasn't entirely true, either, since, physically, they were there. Mentally, not so much.

I stood on wobbly legs, and, this time, Ms. Susan helped me instead of trying to get me to sit down. "You need help."

"I need to get to my brother. Please, come with me to the house. It's closer than an ambulance would be. Please, I need to get back to him."

Her eyes darted around like she was trying to find some sort of answer in the darkness. "He'll need to be seen by a doctor."

"And he will be, but we need to get back to him first. Please, I've left him alone too long already. I need to get back. I need …" I needed to sit down, but I wouldn't do it.

My brother needed me, and I'd get to him.

"We also need Old Man Mosley," I said, trying my best to keep my balance and remember all the jumbled things that were rolling through my mind.

Ms. Susan stood straighter and tilted her head. "Old Man Mosley? Why?"

"He's dead," Bradley said like I should have known it. I did know it, or at least until a few minutes ago, I knew it. Things had changed. I had changed.

"Why do you need him?" Ms. Susan asked without looking at her son.

What? Did she know something?

"Ava, talk to me! The longer you stall, the longer it'll be

before your brother gets help. Why do you need Jacob Mosley?"

She won't believe me. But what do I have to lose?

"Ava?" Bradley prodded.

Fine. "You are going to think I'm crazy, but I need to bring him back to the house."

"Why?" Ms. Susan asked.

"Because his family needs him."

"His family is dead."

"That's why they need him." I looked from Bradley to his mom to gauge their reaction. His mom looked totally calm, like this was something she did every day.

Bradley, on the other hand, looked as pale as a sheet of paper. "Are you telling me there are actual ghosts in Mosley Manor?"

His mom rolled her eyes. "Don't be that way. You know there aren't any ghosts."

"Yeah, but Ava said—"

His mom shooed him off. "Son, I know what Ava said, but she's in shock. Stress can do that to you, especially at such an early and young age. It's also normal for a child to project any changes in the adults around them by thinking they have been possessed or body-snatched.

"I'm not projecting," I said through clenched teeth. "I know exactly what's going on in my house, and I need Old Man Mosley to help me finish it. Do you know where he is or not?"

Ms. Susan hesitated before she nodded at the same time that Bradley answered *he's dead*. Bradley glared at his mother. "You're saying he's not dead?"

"Jacob Mosley died four months ago."

"What?" I gasped, and Bradley ran his fingers through his hair like he couldn't believe what his mom was saying.

"You told me he died twenty years ago!" Bradley challenged.

His mother stood taller, defiant. "To be fair, at the time, the rumor was that he'd died. Then, when I started working at the nursing home in Lindon, I saw him."

"And you didn't think to tell me?" I'd never seen Bradley this irritated.

"Honestly, no. I didn't think you cared about Mr. Mosley or his abandoned house."

"You were wrong," Bradley grumbled.

"I agree." I sided with Bradley.

"What did you want me to say? That the owner, Jacob Mosley, came home after the war to find his brother, sister, and dad dead? Did you want me to tell you that when I was younger, people still thought the house was haunted because Old Man Mosley kept his windows open and talked to himself? Would it have made you feel any better to know that his sister was found in the attic, dead from starvation or her brother, dead from a head injury? Or that Old Man Mosley's father died of a heart attack before help could come for his son? Would any of that have made a difference to you?" She was talking to her son, but I raised my hand to get her attention.

"With all due respect, yes, ma'am, that information would have been very important to me."

Ms. Susan sighed heavily. "Your parents knew, Ava. They knew exactly what they were getting into with your house before they bought it. They didn't care. Said ghost stories weren't true."

We all thought that. We had all learned better.

"Look, I know you kids were scared of him. Kids were scared of Old Man Mosley when I was young, too. But he was just an old man, an old man who constantly talked about needing to go back to the house and take care of his sister and brother. They needed him, or so he thought."

"They did ... they do," I said.

Ms. Susan shook her head. "Don't go believing all that too, Ava. Old Man Mosley was simply a sick man. No more. No less. He lost his family while he was away at war, and he felt guilty ever since. He was too ill to stay in the house by himself, and that's why he was at the nursing home. Then he died. That's why the house finally sold. The bank owned it. I'm sorry, but we can't bring him here."

My legs gave out, and I sat back on the step, my legs numb. If I couldn't get Rachel's older brother to the house to take on her father and make him let them go, then what else could I do? How else could I save my family? This entire thing was so stupid. Why had my parents insisted on buying that house when they could have easily stayed in the rental house next to Bradley's forever?

Why had everything turned upside down?

"Now what?" Bradley asked the million-dollar question.

I looked from him to his mother. His mom had medical knowledge and could take care of Evan. Bradley had ... well, Bradley had moral support. I had determination.

"Now, we go and get my family back."

CHAPTER TWENTY-FIVE

The car ride back to my house was silent, though it sounded to me like I was in a crowded room. All kinds of voices ran through my head, plans I could and couldn't do, how to save Evan, how to save my mom and dad.

I wished I had someone to talk to, someone with experience in the paranormal and supernatural to tell me what to do. I'd read one time in a book next to my seat at the doctor's office that ghosts could be *taken care of* in one of two ways: they could find peace and move on toward the light, or they could be exorcised and forced out. I wanted to try the peaceful way if we could. I saw no need to hurt them if we could help it, even if they were doing a pretty good job of hurting my family—or a few of them were anyway.

The late afternoon sun cast a shadow on the trees out front, leaving mangled and tormented husks in their wake. It was almost poetic, how ominous the house was. Like always, every light in the place was on. I hoped ghosts paid electric bills.

Ms. Susan pulled the car to a stop in front of the house. Bradley shivered like he always did. This time, I joined him.

"Where did you say your brother was?" Ms. Susan asked, surveying the house herself. She had to see the broken top floor window and the dent in the porch where I landed. I wouldn't be able to walk in the morning, but as long as my family was safe, it didn't matter.

"Bathroom. Second floor. Second door on the right." I hoped he was still there.

No, what I hoped was, whatever had happened to my mom and dad had happened to my brother, and he was just playing a part in this stupid echo reenactment of what happened to the Mosley family. Maybe David Mosley had been who Evan had been talking to this entire time, and maybe he'd possessed him, taken him over like my parents had been taken over.

Why hadn't Rachel taken over me?

"We need to get in there," I said the obvious and opened the door.

The warm, humid night hit me as I stepped out of the car. A memory slammed into my brain—the house looked new, the yard perfect. It was a warm night like this with muddy footsteps leading to the house.

I shook my head. "We need inside now." Without waiting for anyone's approval, I ran through the gate and to the front door. It wasn't even locked. They probably expected me to come home.

The house looked exactly as I'd left it. I wasn't sure what I thought would happen. Maybe the paint would turn new, like maybe I'd walk into a time warp, and the house would be brand new.

It wasn't.

It was kind of comforting.

"He's upstairs." I motioned up the stairs for Ms. Susan.

Immediately, she ran up the stairs and disappeared

around the corner. I hoped he was all right. He had to be all right. I couldn't live without him. I didn't want to.

"Welcome back." Rachel's voice surprised me, and I turned toward the living room.

Bradley did the same, and, when he saw her in her full ghostly and see-through form, I thought he was going to pass out. I grabbed him and flinched from my bruises as I tried to hold him up. He wasn't the lightest person in the world, and I wasn't the strongest. Rachel bit her lip, examining us before she disappeared and reappeared just as quickly with a chair from the kitchen in her hand.

"Here." She set it down behind Bradley.

"Th—thanks." His teeth chattered as he sat down in the chair that had been brought to him by a ghost in Mosley Manor. All of his nightmares had to have come true.

"You're welcome." Rachel smiled back. She ran her hands over her apron and appeared in front of me, much too close. "Sorry. I'm not used to this. Been in a mirror for a while. I'm finally free, and I don't know what to do with myself." She took a step back. "Better?"

"Much." I let out a breath and cleared my throat. Okay. It was go time. It was now or never, and it was time to get this done. I wanted my family back. "My plan didn't pan out."

"I'm afraid I don't understand."

And I didn't want to be the one to have to tell her. "Turns out your brother, Jacob, was taken away to live in a nursing home when he could no longer live here. My plan was to get him, bring him back, and have him stand up to your father so he'd let you go."

Her eyes widened and sparkled. "That's brilliant! Oh, my word! I miss him so much. Where is he?"

"Rachel—" How was I supposed to tell her?

She took one look at me; saw how I couldn't even look her in the eyes. "No."

"Rachel, I'm sorry." I could barely get the words out. I knew I needed to hurry, but it didn't feel right to tell her that quickly. I wouldn't want someone to do that to me. She loved Jacob, and he obviously loved her to have kept this house and those memories for so long, even if he hadn't known Rachel was up in the attic the entire time. He'd felt closer to her there, and she, him. It was sad.

It was also time up.

"Rachel!" Mama yelled from the kitchen, and I knew time was most definitely gone. I stepped toward Rachel. If she'd been human … I mean if she'd been solid … I would have reached down and placed my hands on hers for emphasis. As it was, all I could do was look her right in the eyes and hope she got the importance of what I needed her to do.

"Jacob isn't coming to save you." I couldn't help it. My eyes kept glancing at the kitchen doorway and back to Rachel. "You have to help yourself."

She shook her head and backed up. With each word, she backed up a little farther. "What are you saying?"

"I'm saying, your dad has taken over my mom. He's living out your last day or something. I don't know, but I do know that you have to stand up to him."

She shook her head wildly. In her non-solid form, the movement distorted her face. "No, I can't. I can't."

"You can, and you will." How did a person pep talk a ghost?

"Rachel …" Mama called again. This time her voice was deeper, more masculine. Rachel looked at me, terrified.

"He's here."

"He's always been here, hasn't he?" The pieces kept coming together faster and faster. "You didn't stay in the mirror because you had to. You stayed in the mirror because you were afraid of him. Jacob kept him away from you, but you were still scared. You stayed away to protect yourself."

"I stayed away to protect them!" she yelled, surprising both of us. She wiped her nose on the back of her hand and started shaking. "I didn't want to hurt anyone else. I didn't want to hurt Jacob like I'd hurt David."

"You didn't hurt David." I needed her to understand. I needed her to see, to believe it.

"I did. You don't know the whole story. You think you do, but you don't." Rachel looked over her shoulder. Mama stood in the doorway with a sneer curled on her lips. I had to remind myself that wasn't Mama anymore. It was Rachel's father. And he was enjoying this.

"Then tell me, Rachel. Tell me and forgive yourself so you can move on. So your brother can move on. So you can break the hold your father has on you." I wished she was solid, so I could have shaken her. We didn't have time for this. I needed her to face her father, to really face him.

Could she even do that?

"I knew David was playing in the yard. I knew he was in the mud puddle like Father hated, but I did it anyway. I let him do it. I was too busy reading one of my books. Father hated books. Said girls shouldn't read, but I'd taught myself some words, and even if I didn't know all of them, I enjoyed pretending to be somewhere else. That's what I was doing while David played in the mud. I went upstairs to run him a bath, and when I turned around, there he was. Mud and all. Said he heard me calling. I hadn't called. I saw all the muddy footsteps leading to the bathroom, and I lost it." A tear streamed down her face. "I lost it. I yanked him into the bathtub, clothes and all. I washed the hide off him. He screamed and told me to stop, but I was too mad because I knew what Father would do to me. I hadn't paid attention. I'd let my guard down, and my brother died for it."

"Your father died for it, too," Mama said in a deep voice.

I shivered. I wanted my mama back.

Mama took a step toward Rachel, who cowered back toward Bradley and me. I didn't have a chance to check on him. He was still upright, so I imagined he was all right. "After I threw your pathetic self in the attic, I went to check on David. He was already dead. My son. Dead. Dead, because of you, you stupid little girl. I had every intention of coming back up the stairs and making you pay for what you did to my son, but before I could get to the door, my chest felt like it exploded, and I died. Right there on the floor. David tried to leave, but I wouldn't let him. Told him I'd hurt his sister if he did. He loves you very much for some reason." Mama scoffed like she was talking to some peasant. "And you, I couldn't let you leave us here. Not after what you did."

Rachel lowered her head. At this rate, she wouldn't stand up to her father, and we'd all be there forever.

"Where's my dad?" I asked.

"Safe," Mom answered.

"Safe, where?"

She ignored me. She glided slowly toward Rachel with her hands behind her back, like she was a god, looking down on a lowly ant. "I'm never letting you leave this house. Do you understand me? Never."

Rachel lowered her head more and backed up until she was hidden in a corner. Great … just great!

"Ava, we need to get your brother to the hospital now. I tried to call for an ambulance, but my phone wouldn't work." Ms. Susan stopped on the second-to-last step and stared at Mama.

Mama grinned back. Her lips were so twisted and vile that it barely resembled my mother anymore. "I control every-thing in this house," she spat. "Even those useless communi-cation devices."

He really was full of himself.

"What's going on? Why are you talking like this? You

need to be with your son. He's hurt." Ms. Susan tried to reason with my mother. Only my mother wasn't home anymore.

"My son is dead," Mama seethed through her teeth.

"No," Ms. Susan's voice cracked, and, for the first time, she saw what we'd all been seeing. "No, he's not. Evan is alive. And Evan needs help."

"David." Mama let the word drawl in the air. "David is dead. And it's all her fault." Instead of pointing toward Rachel, Mama pointed toward me.

Toward me!

"Wait a second …" I put my hands up to protest whatever she thought I'd done. "I had nothing to do with David. And Rachel didn't, either, if you want to know the truth about it."

Mama scoffed. "The truth? You wouldn't know the truth. You weren't there. But Rachel was. Rachel knows what she did and knows that no matter what you say, she is the reason her brother is dead."

Rachel's father was right about one thing. It was Rachel who held the key to everything. I made a decision, one that I never thought I'd make, but my brother needed help. I didn't want to end up like Rachel. I didn't want to live with all that regret.

Even with Mama's unnaturally blue eyes boring through me, I ran up to Rachel and focused on her. Only on her. "Rachel, you have got to listen to me. My brother is dying. Do you understand me? He needs help. He fell and hit his head, just like your brother did. But you can save him. You can save my brother like you couldn't save yours. Please, fight your father. Make him let us go. Make him let my parents go." A tear fell off my cheek.

Rachel watched it and flinched.

"Please," I whispered. "Please take your life back."

"She won't," Mama chuckled behind me. She was so close

I felt her breath on my neck. Rachel didn't move, though. She kept her eyes on mine. "She knows her place. She knows what she is. She knows what she's done. And she knows that I run this house. I will never let your family go. I won't. You know what? I won't even let the nurse and her sniveling offspring leave, either. You can all stay here with me and rot until the day you die, and then you can be banished to the attic to live out your afterlife."

"You aren't keeping us here!" Bradley's voice boomed through the room, catching us all off guard. He jumped from his seat and, in a fit of bravery, lunged at Mama, at Mr. Mosley. He got one good push in before Mama's hand raised, sending Bradley flying.

"Keep him away from me," Mr. Mosley warned. "Or I will hurt him."

He couldn't hurt Bradley. I couldn't live with myself if he did, same way Rachel couldn't live with what happened to her brother.

"Please," I mouthed to Rachel, my heart pounding in my chest. With everything I had, I willed her to fight off all the fear, all the anger, and face her father. Face him once and for all.

Face him to save Bradley.

Face him to save us all.

"I didn't kill him," she whispered so quietly, even I had a hard time hearing.

It was like she'd been hit with an epiphany. She bit her lip, and her eyes widened just enough for me to see that she'd surprised herself by actually admitting it. "I didn't kill him," she said again, louder.

"You can say it all you want; you know it isn't true." Mama's bass voice rolled against my ear. I didn't blink. I kept my eyes focused on Rachel, giving her all my strength.

"I didn't kill him," she said a bit louder.

"I didn't kill him." A bit louder.

"I didn't kill him!" Louder still. The house shook on its foundation. I didn't look, but I felt Mama back away.

"I didn't kill him!" Rachel yelled.

"I didn't kill him!" The chandelier in the foyer began swinging.

"I didn't kill him!"

Bradley sat up straighter from the floor.

"I didn't kill him!" Rachel looked at me, breathless.

"Now." I blew out a deep, shaking breath. "Tell *him*."

Rachel nodded and stepped around me, facing her father, who had taken over my mother. "I didn't kill him," she repeated.

"So you say, but do you truly believe it?" Mama smirked, but she was weakening. No, she wasn't weakening. Mr. Mosley's hold on her was weakening.

"I was just a child!" Rachel yelled; the windows rattled. "It wasn't my job to take care of David. It wasn't my job to clean up after you when Mama ran away."

"Your mother died," Rachel's father hissed through Mama's lips.

"Mother got tired of you and ran away with another man!" Rachel's entire body shook so fast she blurred. She didn't stop following her father as he backed toward the kitchen with every verbal blow Rachel dealt. "She wanted to take us, but you wouldn't let her."

"She was coming back for us!" I turned toward the stairs, and there was my brother, blood oozing down the back of his head. I knew it wasn't my brother, just like my mother wasn't my mother.

Susan didn't seem to get the idea. "Evan, you need to lie down. You're hurt."

"He's fine," Evan as David said. "He's been a good friend to me. He helped me figure everything out."

"Did he now, son?" Mama snorted. "He manipulated you. And you let him."

"Not anymore. I'm done. I'm done playing your stupid game. Rachel didn't kill me." Evan stepped on the bottom step. "You did."

Rachel's head jerked around. If she could have gotten any paler, she would have. "What?"

"You didn't kill me. I should have told you sooner, but he wouldn't let me." He pointed at Mama, who looked like she wanted to kill them both. "He said if I told you, he'd send you away, away to a bad place. So, I sat in my room and let you think … I'm so sorry."

My brother—Rachel's brother—fell to his knees in front of Rachel. She bent down and laid her non-solid hand to his cheek. "What do you mean?"

"Don't do it," Mama ordered. "I told you what would happen if you did."

Evan looked up. He didn't flinch. Didn't even hesitate. "I'm not afraid of you anymore."

"You should be."

Evan—David—sneered. "No, I shouldn't. But I should apologize forever and ever to you, Rachel. I should never have gotten in the mud. I knew how mad he'd get, but he came home early, remember that?"

She nodded.

"Ever wonder why?"

Rachel nodded again. "But I figured it was for work."

"After he threw you in the attic, he came back in to check on me. Started mumbling about how Mother wanted to come and get us now, with her new husband and her new family. And how he wouldn't let that happen. Ever." Evan/David paused like he was trying to find the right words. "Rachel, yes, I fell and hit my head. There was blood, but I was fine. I would have been fine. Father picked me up. Said Mother couldn't have us … and …"

"And what?" Rachel encouraged.

"And he threw me in the tub. Held me down. Wouldn't let me up. I couldn't breathe. Couldn't get up. My chest hurt. I screamed, and water filled my throat. Then … things got very still …"

Mama stopped in her tracks. All the air left the room. Even Bradley sat up and listened.

"He killed David?" I asked once the words finally formed.

Mama's face contorted into something that didn't even resemble her. It was ugly and monstrous. It was Mr. Mosley. Mama's body fell to the floor as Mr. Mosley, in ghost form, stood straight and tall. He fixed the cuffs of his shirt, seemingly unfazed by the truth that had come out. He had slicked-back, black hair, a long mustache that had been curled up on the sides, and a black business suit.

I ran over to Mama to make sure she was okay. I cared about the Mosley drama; I did. But I cared about Mama more. She was breathing, thank goodness. She'd be okay. I knew she would.

We'd get out of this.

"I did what I had to do. To keep their mother" —he said the word like it was the most disgusting word ever— "from having them. And I still have them." He laughed. "And I'll always have them.

Rachel was doubled over like she'd been kicked in the stomach. "All these years, I hated myself. I thought I'd killed him." She wasn't speaking to anyone in particular. She paced in a circle. I didn't know what she was thinking, but I imagined it had something to do with all the time she'd spent over the last century thinking she'd killed her brother. How lonely she'd been. How she was afraid of her father even when her older brother had been there to protect her.

"Because you are a girl," her father grumbled. "And you are gullible."

Rachel stood straighter. Fire burned in her eyes, not literal fire, but anyone could tell she'd finally had enough. "Get out of this house." Her words were shaky, but the intent was there.

"Make me." He yawned. He actually yawned.

"Get out of this house!" she screamed, and the walls shivered. Mama held onto me, and I held onto her. Bradley's mother had bent down and was hugging Bradley, who looked like he wanted to throw up. I felt the same.

Mr. Mosley staggered back just a bit but recovered and pulled his coat down like he hadn't been affected. "No. It's my home."

Rachel had enough. "Actually, it's the Kirkland home! And they want you to leave."

Wind picked up inside the house. Papers and dust flew through the air, and the curtains billowed on the curtain rods.

"They want you to leave!" Rachel repeated. She didn't stutter. Not one little bit. They want you to leave. And I want you to leave. You don't have control over me anymore!"

When she said the words, a red light burst from the fireplace. It engulfed her father, who, for the first time, actually looked terrified. He screamed for her to help him, but she didn't move a muscle. Neither did David, who had stepped outside of Evan. Evan laid on the floor in a heap. Mama and I hurried over to him, and I pulled him into my lap.

With one last scream, Mr. Mosley disappeared into the bright red light, never to be seen again.

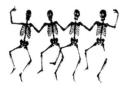

CHAPTER TWENTY-SIX

Everything that had been flying around the room fell in an instant. It would be one more mess to clean up, but it was worth it. Everything had worked out. I had Mama and Evan back.

"Guys?" Daddy came out of the study; most likely, he'd been in the bedroom the entire time. Some people had all the luck.

"Daddy!" I ran to him and pulled him into a hug. I didn't care that my ribs hurt so bad. I wanted my dad. I never wanted to let him go.

"What's this all about?" he asked, rubbing my hair gently.

"Glad you're you, that's all." I flinched at the pain radiating through my side, but I hugged him tighter anyway. Mama joined behind me, my brother on the side. Our family was back together. We were ourselves again, and I couldn't ask for anything more.

"Jacob!" Rachel squealed, breaking our little family hug up.

A bright white light lit up the middle of the living room.

In it, a young man stood in an army uniform. It had to have been Jacob in his younger days. Interesting that he didn't look like he did when he died like Rachel did.

"Who's that?" Daddy pointed to the larger glowing, obviously ghostly form of a man in our living room. Guess I had to believe in ghosts after everything that happened and everything I'd seen. Part of my identity, gone.

"That … that's a family waiting too long to be together." I laid my head on Mama's shoulder, watching as the people, spirits, surrounded in white light, saw each other for the first time in decades.

"Ghosts aren't real." Bradley's mama inched closer to us, holding a dazed Bradley up under his arm. He'd looked better.

"Tell them that." I motioned toward Jacob, who was glowing.

"I knew it!" Bradley, whose head was still bleeding and would need to see a doctor soon, nearly jumped up and down from his excitement. "Ghosts are real! Take that, Ava!"

"Yes," I sighed with a hint of a smile. "Looks like you were right."

I'd never seen Bradley smile that big or be so proud of himself. I supposed he deserved it. Just this once.

"Rachel? My Rachel!" Jacob beamed, holding out his arms toward his sister.

Giggling, Rachel ran toward her brother and jumped into his arms. He hugged her tightly, burying his face into her hair. I couldn't see Jacob's face, but I imagined tears streamed down his face.

Tears streamed down Mama's cheeks.

I might have shed a tear as well.

"Jacob!" David ran like a blur and joined his brother and sister in a circle, much like my family.

"I finally have my family." Jacob kissed both of his siblings on the top of their heads. "You ready to go home?"

Rachel looked at David. At first, her expression was blank. Then, her face lit up like a Christmas tree. "Of course we are, silly."

Holding on to her brother's arm for dear life, Rachel took the time to address me. "Thank you, Ava."

"Of course." I waved, but there was just one more thing. "My friend, Gracie. She saw you in the attic, and it really freaked her out. Do you think she'll be okay?"

Rachel narrowed her eyes. "That wasn't me. That was the other ghost in the attic, Meredith. You didn't think we were the first or only ones, did you? She didn't like Gracie. Too judgy."

Other ghost?

Bradley's smug expression washed away.

Another ghost …

"Wait …" I wanted answers, but the light that surrounded the Mosley family grew brighter and brighter.

"Thank you, again," Rachel yelled through the light. "Thank you for giving me my family back."

And just like that, they were gone.

"That … what just … what?" Daddy pointed to where the ghosts had been.

"This place really was haunted." Susan doubled over and put her hands on her knees, sucking in a lot of air.

"Is," I corrected, thinking about Meredith in the attic. I hoped she didn't have a terrible, horrible backstory that could come back and bite us.

"Is," Bradley repeated and turned a very unflattering color of green.

Susan sucked in a deep breath and straightened her shoulders. "Okay. So, there are ghosts … ghosts in this house …

That's … you can deal with that. Now, I should get Bradley to the hospital. And I think you should get Ava checked out."

"Yeah, take Bradley. He looks super horrible."

"Thanks," he deadpanned.

"Well, you do. Talk to you later."

"Later." He hobbled out, holding onto his mom. I hoped he was okay. I hoped he'd call me soon. So much hope.

So … much … pain.

Ouch.

"Sweetie, are you okay?" My dad placed his hands on each side of my face, checking me for any injuries.

"I'll live." Though I saw a doctor visit in my future. "Check on Mama."

So he did.

"I don't honestly know what happened. I feel a bit dizzy. Who were … where did they go? Ava, do you know?" Mama looked around the room, ignoring Daddy's close inspection of her possible injuries.

Seemingly content that Mama was more or less okay, Daddy pulled her into a huge kiss. Looked like with Mr. Mosley gone, the evil presence had lifted, and everyone was back to themselves.

"What do you think about that?" I pulled Evan aside and let Mama and Daddy have their reunited moment.

"I think I hope Meredith is a nice ghost." Evan pulled me into a hug and kissed my cheek. I couldn't remember the last time Evan had kissed me. I wiped it up as quickly as he'd placed it, but secretly, I was glad to have him back.

"I think I hope we move," I countered. I seriously didn't want to stay in this house any longer.

"Oh, come on," Mama teased, her head resting on Daddy's arm. They looked as sickeningly sweet as they used to look before we moved here. I loved it! "It has good bones."

"Bones literally buried under the foundation. Probably Meredith's." Evan shivered.

More than likely.

But it didn't matter if we moved or stayed. Wherever we were, wherever we went, we'd be family. Forever and ever … and beyond.

ACKNOWLEDGMENTS

I want to thank everyone at Monster Ivy for believing in this book. Your enthusiasm is appreciated more than you know.

Cammie, your cover is amazing! I'm in love.

Tia, thank you for reading this book and making it so much better.

Rachel, I'm sorry for any nightmares I might have caused ... (mostly).

I want to thank God for putting me on this wild ride. It's amazing to put stories in the world.

And thank you, hi, for reading this book.

—Kelly Martin, 1/5/2020

ABOUT THE AUTHOR

Kelly Martin lives in a possibly haunted house in a small Southern town. While she'd like to say paranormal things have only happened to her at her home, it would be a lie ...

She is an active member of the Horror Writers Association and an international #1 best selling author in horror, paranormal, contemporary, historical, young adult, and mysteries. All of Kelly's books have one thing in common—imagine the real world is tilted slightly on its side. You don't really know what's going on, what's missing, but there is a tilt, a hum you can barely hear, telling you that something is off.

Email Kelly Martin at kelly@kellymartinbooks.com (no spaces).

Want to know about new releases, chat with Kelly, go behind the scenes on all her books? Find out how here: https://linktr.ee/kellymartinauthor.

Keep your ghostly adventure going with *Dark and Deadly Things* (book 1 in the Haunted House series). Full series out now.

TRINITY ROW

CHAPTER 1

If it's as dead on the inside as it is on the outside, we're all screwed.

My mom and I arrived at the house known as Trinity Row a few minutes ago, and so far, we haven't spoken to each other.

We haven't looked at each other.

We haven't taken our eyes off the house.

A few pieces of ancient cement from what would be a stretch to call a sidewalk crumble under my heels, and I have to stagger back to catch myself on the side of the truck. I always thought our '05 Chevy was old. Looking at this house, clearly, I have the definition of *old* wrong.

"Well . . . hmmm . . ." Mama is speechless, or rather she has words, but words she'd rather not say in front of me. Trinity Row is a new venture for us. I'm sure she doesn't want to scare me off any more than I already am. Oh, I'm scared, all right.

Jane is a liar.

This was supposed to be the easy house. One to make us

money so we could move on to bigger and better things, or, at the very least, move to the next town and try to forget.

Moving would be the easy part. Forgetting would never happen.

"I mean . . . it's standing." That's about all Trinity Row is, standing. I'm sure back in its time it stood beautifully. It reminds me of one of those Southern Gothic houses, the ones with turrets and balconies and all sorts of unnecessary decorations that made it the envy of all the neighbors. I imagine old women sitting on the large wrap-around front porch, breaking green beans while chatting about the latest gossip in Lawrence. I'm sure children played in the bright green grass in the front yard. Everything had been ideal. Everything had been perfect.

Until the twentieth century happened.

I'm sure tragedy struck. People died. Souls were left behind. Bad things happened. The house decayed. The bodies inside decayed.

And now we're here to fix it up and sell it.

I see nothing that can go wrong here.

Especially since it's no longer a grand Southern Gothic princess. Its heyday disappeared with the horse and buggy. Two towers reach toward the sky, making the house look taller than the two stories Mama said it was. The second seems to be bulking a bit outward, and the first is tilted ever so slightly on its side. All the windows are boarded up except for one on the second floor, where one lone, lace, dingy-looking curtain blows in the fall breeze seeping in from broken glass. Brown grass as tall as my knee fills the patch of land surrounding Trinity Row haphazardly, contained only by a rusted metal fence surrounding the property on three sides. The other side is held together by a falling wooden fence that appears to have been painted white sometime in the Washington era.

All the other houses around the neighborhood are brick and look fairly the same—one story, probably built in the mid-70s, large trees in the yard, curtains closed in the picture windows.

Every other house on this street looks to be alive—hiding, but alive.

Nothing about Trinity Row is alive.

"Jane is supposed to meet us here at three," says Mama. "We're about ten minutes early." Jane is someone Mama knows who called out of the blue and asked if she'd like to buy Trinity Row. Mama, in a fit of insanity, said yes.

And here we are.

"To be fair, we've been driving ten hours, Mama." To be fair, *she's* been driving for ten hours. I've been pretending to be asleep. It helps cover that awkward silence that unfortunately happens on long trips. There's only so much small talk a person can get through before the real important topics of conversation inevitably sneak in. I'm not ready to talk about the real important topics of conversation. Neither is she. So, we have infinite small talk.

At least it gets us through the day.

I hope it gets us through this renovation.

"So, we are really going to live here while we renovate?" 'Cause I'm not even sure the floor will hold us up. The porch might collapse before we make it that far.

"It's no worse than the house in Camden," she counters, giving me the side-eye. She totally knows this house is worse than the house in Camden. Though not by much. "Okay, it is, but Jane assured me that it's safe to live in."

"I thought it was condemned."

"It is . . . kinda. But look, this house was a dollar. One dollar! We can renovate it and sell it. We can use that money to buy a house of our own. Wouldn't that be nice? To not have to run—not have to move so much."

My chest tightens. I knew what she stopped herself from saying. She was going to say to not have to run like we had been. I can't say that I want to stop running. I will say that if she wants to stop, then I will . . . but only for her.

"Who knows, maybe Lawrence, Tennessee, is just the place to settle?" She gives me an awkward side-hug. Neither of us has worked out exactly how we're supposed to act around each other now. At least we're trying. More than I can say for my dad. He left about six months after *the incident*. He told Mama it was either me or him. She chose me.

She chose wrong.

"Don't go that far," I tease lightly and smile. It feels nice to smile. My cheeks will hurt in the morning. I can't remember the last time I smiled and the smile not be forced to make Mama feel better.

She pats me on the shoulder and grabs her duffel bag from the back seat. "Let's see what we've got."

What we've got is a mess. I could tell her that without going through the motions. This is our third house renovation in three years. I love doing it. The renovating is fun and knocking down walls is therapeutic. Making something pretty out of something ugly is good for the soul. However, there's renovation, and there's whatever we're doing at Trinity Row. It will most definitely be our biggest job yet.

Again, Jane is a liar.

I think Mama is up to the challenge, though. It's when she looks the most alive.

I grab my bag, too, and follow Mama through the old latch gate, which reminds me of the one we had at the cemetery in Jasper. It's a few miles up the road, where our original road trip started. I never want to go back there. Of course, I never wanted to come back to Tennessee, either, but here I am. Home sweet home.

The walkway to the porch crumbles under each step, just like the sidewalk did. Good thing Mama paid only a dollar for this place. I have a feeling it'll take most of our savings to pay for the renovation. I know she's hoping for a big return. We'll have to make it look less like a haunted attraction for that to happen.

Optimism!

Mama leads the way, surveying the house with every step she takes. I'm sure she already has color scheme ideas flooding her mind. She probably even has an open house date all planned out. Planning is what keeps her sane. I didn't inherit that gene. My brother did.

Right when she puts her foot on the first step, a scream bellows so loud, a murder of black birds erupts from their roost behind the house and have a flying tizzy toward the sky. They squawk and flap their wings frantically, until all of them have disappeared toward town.

Mama grabs my arm and spins me around until I'm behind her on the first step, blocking me from whatever made that noise. She holds me back, her hand on my waist, keeping me from moving, protecting me from whatever is coming our way.

The screams turn into words, one word actually— repeated. "No . . . no . . . no . . . no!"

I peek over Mama's shoulder. A man, he must be in his eighties, stumbles and trips up the walkway toward us. His blue, cataract-covered eyes are frantic, scared, terrified —terrifying.

His white hair flies around his head. "No! No!" He points his crooked finger in our direction. It shakes violently. I'm not sure if it's because of us or if he has a disease that has affected his body—and his mind.

"Sir, sir, calm down. My name is Amber Black. This is my

daughter, Ivy. We bought this house. We're supposed to be here. We're going to fix it up, so hopefully some nice family can move in. Wouldn't that be lovely?" Mama's voice is calm, but shaky. She's still holding onto me, her fingers digging into my skin through my coat.

Her reassurances only make things worse. "No!" he yells louder, stumbling over his feet and falling to his knees. It doesn't stop him. Instead of running toward us, he crawls.

"S-sir," Mama stutters, caught between helping him and her primal need to protect me. She shouldn't worry about me so much.

A bloody trail forms behind him the closer he gets to us. The sidewalk is scraping his palms and cutting into the thin skin of his knees.

"Maybe we should go?" I whisper in Mama's ear. Obviously, this man doesn't want us here, for whatever reason, and if he's this determined, then maybe we should listen. I don't want to be somewhere I'm not wanted, and I don't want to be somewhere that doesn't want me.

Trinity Row doesn't want me? That's totally fine. I'm not attached to it in the slightest.

"No!" is the only word I can understand. He's mumbling incoherently as he crawls toward us.

Mama lets me go and reaches into her pocket. "I'm going to call for help, sir. I'm going to get someone to help you."

Before she gets the phone to her ear, a young man, he looks to be around my age, runs from around the house, falls to his knees, and grabs the old man by the shoulders. "Stop," he orders, his voice calm but demanding.

The old man's eyes widen, and he shakes, looking the younger man in the eyes.

"Do you remember me?" the young man asks.

The old man places his palm slowly on the younger man's

face. He cups his arthritis-battered fingers around the younger man's cheek and rubs it gently, lovingly. He nods.

"Good." The younger man sounds happy. He pats the older man on the shoulder a few times, a silent understanding falling between them. I wonder who they are and how they know each other. Mainly, I want to know why the older dude wants Mama and me out of Trinity Row. If he knows something I don't, I'm all ears.

The younger man clears his throat. "Look, you don't belong here, right? You need to leave . . ."

"No," he grunts, shaking wildly.

The younger man holds onto the older man. "Yes, West. Yes. Listen to me, okay?"

"No." West, I assume his name is West, pushes the younger man back. He doesn't budge.

The younger man reaches for the other man's hands. "West, stop it! You're going to hurt yourself. Calm down. They're fine."

"No!" West moves to the side, and when the younger man follows him, West ducks to the side and gets away. His eyes frantic and his movements stiff, the old man crawls toward us again; a guttural yell fills the air.

"No, West, stop!" The younger man staggers in front of the older one. Again, the younger man puts his hands on the older man's shoulders to stop him. West pushes a time or two, but it is obvious that exhaustion is winning.

When it seems West has no fight left in him, the young man gently brushes the hair back from the old man's sweaty forehead and pushes it behind his ear. "It's okay. I promise. I'll make sure everything is all right. I'll take care of it. You need to trust me. Remember?"

The old man hesitates and whimpers.

"West, remember?"

The old man breathes in a few times, deep breaths, and places his age-worn hands on the younger man's hands. He pats them a few times and nods.

"Good," the younger man says shakily. "Good. You need to go home now."

Fear fills the old man's eyes, and he points toward Mama and me.

The younger man finally turns toward us, and for the first time, I can actually see who has been trying to protect us—or rather protect the old man.

Sky blue eyes, almost the same color as the old man's, are the first things I notice. They are piercing, handsome, beautiful. They draw me in, and I have to fight to focus on something else. His hair is a nice distraction: dark brown, slightly curly, and flops in his eyes. He has on dark blue jeans and a white T-shirt that has sleeves that are a bit too tight for his muscles. It's chilly today, and despite that, he doesn't have on a jacket. I'm cold just looking at him. "It's okay, West, I'll take care of them. Don't you worry." He turns back toward the other man. "Go home, okay? It's good to see you."

West gives us a weary look, like there is some sort of battle going on in his mind. He opens his mouth to say something but closes it just as quickly. Whatever it is, I guess he thinks Mama and I don't need to know. I'm not so sure about that.

The dark-haired guy helps West to the gate and whispers something in his ear before pulling him into a quick hug, and then sending him on his way.

Once West is across the road, the dark-haired man turns on his heels and strides confidently toward us. When he gets a few feet away, he smiles a smile that would make the angels think lustful thoughts. I know I do, even though I shouldn't. Deep dimples cut into his cheeks, making him look completely innocent and completely dangerous all at the same time.

"My name is John. Welcome to Trinity Row."

*ENJOY THE AUDIOBOOK OR CONTINUE READING AT ANY BOOK RETAILER ONLINE.